"It seems like just yesterday that Laura was your age," says Gran, smiling down at me. "You remind me of her so much. Imogen looks more like her, but your personality is so similar to your mum's. You have her sense of humor and her sense of fairness. You're a wonderful listener, just like your mother. I'll never stop missing Laura, but at least I get to see glimpses of her every day in you and your sister."

I squeeze Gran's hand, not sure how to respond. That's why people think I'm a good listener, not because I am but because I often don't know what to say.

"Someone at the hospice told me that grief is like glitter," Gran says.

"If you throw a handful of glitter in the air, even if you try your very best to clean it up, you'll never get it all. I think that's true. I keep finding glitter tucked into unexpected corners. I suppose it will always be there."

I lie in bed that night pondering Gran's grief glitter. It's true. There are little piles of it waiting to be found everywhere.

Also by Yvette Clark
The House Swap

GLITTER

gets

EVERYWHERE

YVETTE CLARK

HARPER
An Imprint of HarperCollinsPublishers

Library of Congress Control Number: 2021930847
ISBN 978-0-06-303449-5

Typography by Jessie Gang
22 23 24 25 26   PC/BRR   10 9 8 7 6 5 4 3 2 1
❖
First trade paperback edition, 2022

* ★ *

For Abel, Beatrice, and Gabriel, who give me
love and laughter every single day

* ★ *

GLITTER

gets

EVERYWHERE

CHAPTER ONE

WAITING AT THE WINDOW

I can't decide if today is the second or third worst day of my life. Perhaps half past ten in the morning is too early to tell. It is the most terrible Friday and the saddest rainy day ever. The absolute worst day of my life was an inappropriately sunny Tuesday earlier this week. I know that for sure. The other contender for second place was the day a few months ago when I fully understood the unbearable truth of what was going to happen.

The London street below my window is wet, gray, and deserted on this March morning. I check the Farrow & Ball color chart taped to my wall. There are hundreds of different colors of paint, and fifty-five of them are shades of white and cream. My eyes search for the perfect match until they land on color number 272, Plummett. How perfect, as I have plummeted here to land at my window seat, the fall so fast that my stomach is in my throat, and my ears hurt.

The cherry trees on our street are finally blooming, their flowers arriving just in time to say hello and good-bye to Mum. Their pale-pink blossoms, color number 245, Middleton Pink, are lapping up the rain.

If it weren't raining, I'd like to go to the park with my best friend, Jessica, but she'll be at school today along with everyone else. I wish that I were there, sitting at my desk next to her while we try to conjugate French verbs under the watchful eye of Madame Olivier. Jessica's mum is coming today, but she said that Jess is "far too young, Kitty, dear," even though she's the same age as me. When Jessica left yesterday, she squeezed my hand so tightly that her nails left little crescent-moon-shaped indents in my skin, which were still there when I went to bed.

Mum always smiled on rainy days like this one, closing her eyes and tilting her face to the heavens. She hardly ever used an umbrella, preferring instead to wear a sky-blue raincoat with a hood that was forever blowing down. Mum said that the rain is like a beauty treatment from nature, so why would you want to cover your face? Dad would mutter that it was nice weather for ducks, and grab his enormous black umbrella, determination to stay dry between home, train station, and office written on his face.

Dad hasn't been to work for nearly two weeks now.

I don't usually like the rain, but today this endless London drizzle suits me just fine. My sister, Imogen, said that when the weather reflects a character's mood in a book or poem, it's called pathetic fallacy, or something like that. She's thirteen and knows everything, or thinks she does. I'm ten and know that I don't. According to Imogen when I'm her age, I still won't know the things she does because she got the looks *and* the brains in the family. When I asked Mum what I got, she smiled at me.

"Kitty, you have your own looks and brains, no better or worse than your sister's, but just perfect for you."

Well, that was definitely a lie, because it's a fact that Imogen is prettier than me, and everyone knows it. I have a bump on my nose, and people often ask me how I broke it. I didn't! Imogen's nose is perfect. Dad said that "physical perfection can lack character," but he was just saying that a) to make me feel better, and b) because his nose is identical to mine.

Imogen has long silky honey-colored hair, and bright-blue eyes just like Mum's. Her hair hangs to the middle of her back, covering her bra strap. The fact that she wears a bra and that her locks reach it are two more ticks in the Imogen column. She looks as if she belongs in California with sun, surfers, and palm trees, rather than in this leafy part of North London. Imogen is the beauty of the family, and I, while not quite the beast, am definitely the plain Jane. I have dull brown hair cut neatly into a blunt chin-length bob, which the paint chart pronounces an exact match for color number forty, Mouse's Back. My eyes are the same rodent color as my hair. I can run faster than my sister though, and I'm going to be taller. I'm catching up already.

I press my burning cheek against the cool window and study the street below, but there's nothing to see; only the cars parked outside their houses tell of the existence of my neighbors. Instead, I look down at the itchy navy-blue pleated skirt I'm wearing, purchased on a miserable shopping trip the day before. I wanted a black top to wear with the skirt, but Gran said no.

"Black is not a color for children, Kitty. Anyway, navy and black would make you look like a bruise."

"I feel like a bruise," I replied, which made Gran's face soften slowly, eventually crumpling in on itself like a paper bag. She turned away, and I quickly shoved the black sweater back on the shelf and picked up the navy one. I trailed after Gran through the store until we arrived at the cash register, where she paid in silence.

"Kitty, love, the car's going to be here soon," Dad calls up the stairs. "Are you ready to go?"

Of course I'm not ready. How could I ever be ready for this? I touch the silver heart on the charm bracelet Mum gave to me a few weeks ago. The solitary charm looks almost as lonely as I feel. Imogen had been given the same bracelet and charm. We aren't sure where or when Mum had bought them. I suppose she must have ordered them online. We don't know if she gave anything to Dad, and we won't ever ask him. There's so much we don't know. Mum also left a pile of letters in thick cream envelopes for Imogen and me to read on our next three birthdays. The envelopes are decorated with drawings of flowers, love hearts, and sunshines, with our name and age written in the middle in Mum's curly handwriting. Three letters just aren't enough. I'll only be thirteen when I get the last one. Why did Mum think it was okay to stop the letters then? What about when I'm eighteen, or twenty-five, thirty-seven, fifty-two, or even seventy? Some people still get letters from their mums at that age. When Dad showed us the six envelopes, I asked him why there were only three each. He put his head in his hands and spoke so quietly that I could barely make out the words.

"She had to stop writing, love. There was no more time."

Maybe he hadn't spoken at all but just sighed out one single, sad breath. He didn't notice when I crept out of the kitchen and upstairs to my room. Lying awake in bed that night I realized that Imogen had three extra years with Mum. This thought ticked back and forth in my brain like a metronome and gave me a headache. It took me ages to get to sleep.

Through the window, I see a large, glossy black car turning onto the street. It looks as if it might not fit, and it crosses my mind how awkward it would be if it scraped one of the neighbors' cars, setting off their alarm in a shrill wailing. It's a very posh car, much fancier than our old Volvo, which is parked forlornly outside. Mum had planned to get an environmentally friendlier car called a Prius, but that doesn't matter anymore. Nobody's going to care now about the carbon emissions of our old Volvo. This black shiny monster gliding toward my house is definitely not good for the environment and Mum would hate it. I hope she isn't in a car like this one. She's probably already at the church, waiting silently for us to arrive.

Saint Stephen's Church is where Mum and Dad got married and where Imogen and I were christened. Imogen was a pink, frilly flower girl at their wedding. She apparently took ages to walk down the aisle, because she was trying to do pointy ballet toes while she scattered clouds of rose petals. Mum was five months pregnant with me on their wedding day, so I actually walked down the aisle with her, tucked neatly under her billowing ivory dress. I've always wanted to be a real bridesmaid, but I don't care anymore. I wouldn't do it now even if someone asked me, and they probably will because everyone feels sorry for me.

It's time to go.

CHAPTER TWO

AT THE CHURCH

Hampstead High Street is bustling with locals and tourists who crowd the narrow sidewalks despite the rain. People must think we are in a wedding car, as several shoppers smile and wave at us enthusiastically during our slow drive up the treelined hill, eliciting tut-tutting and vigorous eye-rolling from Gran. They peer into the car as we wait at the traffic lights, their grins disappearing as they take in the black-clad, red-eyed occupants. People turn away wishing they had never seen us.

It isn't even that far to the church from our house. We should have walked. Mum would have preferred that. She liked to walk everywhere, dragging us in her wake. It's one and a half miles from our house to Gran's, and providing the weather was fine, and we had the time, we always walked there and back. Fine weather for Mum was anything that didn't involve torrential rain, thunder, or lightning.

When we arrive at the ancient church, the car glides into a miraculously empty parking space, directly in front of the gate. I wonder if someone put traffic cones out there so we'd have a place to park when we arrived, and then discreetly whisked them away as we turned the corner. The vicar is waiting under his huge umbrella to greet us. He smiles kindly at Imogen and me and shakes hands and speaks softly with Dad and Gran.

It's so quiet inside the church that our footsteps echo embarrassingly as we walk to the front pew to take our seats. It's gloomy too, as the church is lit only by dozens of flickering candles and the gray light that is seeping in through the stained-glass windows. When I twist around in my seat, I see the church is full. Although I recognize lots of faces, there are just as many people I don't know. Who are they all, and how did they know my mum? Whenever I catch someone's eye they give me a small, sad smile and hold my gaze, as if to turn away from a child's sadness would be shameful, but I wouldn't blame them at all if they did.

Somebody must have given me the order of service as I entered the church because I'm clutching it in my hands. According to the card, the song the choir is currently singing is called "Make Me a Channel of Your

Peace." We'd worked together on the program for the funeral, or memorial, as we were supposed to be calling it—the least fun family activity imaginable. Imogen and I were allowed to choose the picture of Mum for the front cover, and for once we were in total agreement, not a single argument; there was just one photo we both wanted. The photograph had been taken in my godmother Kate's garden before cancer became part of my family. It was already there though, hiding malevolently behind Mum's radiant smile, an unwelcome and uninvited guest. In the photo, Mum is gazing squarely at the camera half laughing, her nose crinkled up and her grass-green dress blowing around her legs. She is so healthy and full of life in the picture, so very different from the way she looked over the last few months. I turn the card over in my lap because it makes my heart hurt even more to see her longed-for face. The back of the order of service is mercifully blank. Just like my mum, I realize, here and then not, everything and then nothing. How can that be? I start to think about what I wouldn't give to have her back with me, but stop because it's scary.

Imogen and I are wedged tightly in between Dad and Gran, even though they have space on either side of them. Nobody else has chosen to sit with us in this pew. Attending a funeral is the opposite of going to a concert or the theater. At a funeral, nobody wants to sit at the front. It's better to be at the back—the farther away you are, the less it hurts. Imogen is staring furiously into her lap, her fingers folding and unfolding the fabric of her dress. How come she was allowed to wear black? Dad and Gran are alternating between looking at us and looking at the coffin, which is already in position at the front of the church, just as Mum had wanted. My sister and I did a lot of listening at doors over the past few months. As Mum got more and more ill, our ears were pressed closer and closer to doors and walls. Our parents tried to include us in the funeral planning. In Mum's professional opinion, she probably thought it was healthy to involve us. This particular detail, however, I had eavesdropped a few weeks ago.

"Rob, there is absolutely no way I want you and a bunch of our friends carrying me down the same aisle I walked down to marry you. It's incredibly morbid. I think it's more appropriate if I'm there when everyone arrives."

"Appropriate? Maybe if we imagine that you'll be hosting the world's most tragic cocktail party, then yes, it's appropriate," said Dad.

"Rob, I agree with Laura," said Gran. "It is in fact quite dignified to be there, waiting for the mourners to arrive. I wonder why more people don't do it that way. I always worry one of the pallbearers is going to trip and drop the coffin, and probably in this case it would be your idiotic friend Dominic. He always was a clumsy oaf. Do you remember how he spilled red wine all over me at your wedding? I never did get the stain out of that lovely trouser suit."

As she so often did, Gran settled the matter. Or maybe Dad thought there was a reasonable chance that Dominic might drop the coffin. Either way, there was no further discussion, and so there Mum lay when we arrived, gently waiting. I hate to think of her in that box. Her actual body is lying there at the front of the church, and she is entirely on her own. I start to shake, Dad pulls me closer into him, and the service begins.

Most of the next forty-five minutes are a blur. Everything that the vicar says gets lost in the space between his mouth and my ears. I miss Kate's reading entirely, but when Dad walks up to the front of the church, I sit up, stick straight, and hold my breath. He stands there for a long moment leaning against the lectern, his face tired and pale, and his hair too long. His suit, shirt, and tie are pristine, in stark contrast to the body inhabiting them. When he speaks, his voice is surprisingly loud, clear, and comforting, as if he is there to make the rest of us feel a bit better.

"Laura asked me to read this poem to you today. As you know, she loved poetry, and when she found this piece she knew right away it was what she wanted to share with all of you:

> "I give you this one thought to keep.
> I am with you still. I do not sleep.
> I am a thousand winds that blow.
> I am the diamond glints on the snow.
> I am the sunlight on ripened grain.
> I am the gentle autumn rain.
> When you awake in the morning's hush,
> I am the swift, uplifting rush
> Of quiet birds in circled flight.
> I am the soft stars that shine at night
> Do not think of me as gone.
> I am with you still in each new dawn."

I mouth the words along with Dad. The poem is printed out in the order of service, but I don't need to look at the words. I know every line by heart. I asked Mum to read it to me over and over again after she'd chosen it so that I could hear her voice in my head at this exact moment. My sister must have taken my hand, or maybe I reached for hers, since our fingers are entwined. I know that Imogen, like me, can hear Mum's voice speaking the words along with Dad. I think about the woman who wrote the poem and who she might have written it for, all those years ago. I bet she was a mother too. I can imagine her sitting beside a stream, beneath a weeping willow tree, conjuring these words to comfort the family she had to leave behind. Mum said we only needed to remember five of the words and that they'll always be true—"I am with you still." I can't feel her, though.

CHAPTER THREE

LIGHT RELIEF

"Thank goodness that's over!" exclaims Kate, enveloping me and my tear-soaked face in caramel-colored cashmere and a cloud of perfume that tickles the back of my throat. Kate's usually immaculate makeup is smeared, with small pale tear trails down her cheeks and dark smudges under her eyes. I suppose nobody is looking their best today, despite having dressed carefully for the occasion. Gran sent Imogen to the loo with her friend Lily to try to remove her black eyeliner, which has left inky-looking streaks on her face.

"Let me look at my beautiful goddaughter," Kate says, leaning back to examine my pink blotchy cheeks. She tucks a stray strand of hair behind one ear. "Yes, just as gorgeous as ever, and so brave. How are you feeling, my darling?"

Kate's right, it is a relief that the funeral is over. Now,

though, there's a strange anticlimactic feeling, almost as if you've finished an exam you've been dreading, but as you know that you failed miserably, there is no celebration.

"I'm all right." I sniff loudly, taking the proffered white cotton hankie, my own long since drenched with tears and snot and stuffed into Dad's jacket pocket. "Do you know when Dad will get to the reception?"

Gran told me it is called a wake, not a reception, but that sounds weird to me—like you are waiting for the person you love to wake up. Gran said I was being silly, and it's called that because people used to stay awake all night and sit with the body. I'm glad we didn't have to do that.

"I think he said that they'd be about an hour. Knowing Dominic, he'll have his hip flask with him and give your dad some on the way there. Speaking of which, I could really do with a gin and tonic."

Dad and Dominic had gone straight from the church to take Mum to Golders Green Crematorium. Dominic's going because he's been Dad's best friend since primary school and Mum knew he would need someone there with him. She didn't want Imogen or me to go to the crematorium and asked Gran and Kate to stay with us, so it's only Dad and Dominic who'll be there for the last part of the funeral. I know what the crematorium looks like from the outside because we used to take the number thirteen bus past it on our way home from summer outings to Golders Hill Park. It looks like a church, although I found out that the tall tower houses the chimney rather than bells, which is a truly awful thought and something that I wish I didn't know. Mum told us that the gardens are beautiful, with a lily pond and hundreds of crocuses. It's where the shrink Sigmund Freud, a famous ballerina named Anna Pavlova, the author Enid Blyton, and our own grandpa were cremated, as well as hundreds of thousands of other people. Mum was always very matter-of-fact about life and death, and when she told us these things, we found them interesting rather than frightening.

I saw a cremation on television once. The coffin glided slowly down a conveyor belt to be incinerated. There were deep-purple silk curtains, which closed after the coffin slid past, while creepy organ music played, and then nothing, no more music, and no more body. After seeing the cremation on TV, I decided I would rather be buried, but Imogen told me that worms and insects eat your body, and that would be much worse. I did some research online and discovered that even with a metal-lined coffin, the creepy-crawlies can still get in, although I'm not sure how. It seems as if there are no good options. Perhaps someone will have invented one by the time I die. Imogen suggested being dropped into a pool of green acid, which she said she'd seen in a James Bond film, but that person had been alive at the time! Dad told her off for scaring me. I think Mum picked the best option available, but I'm relieved not to have to see the curtains close or to drive away from the crematorium in the shadow of that chimney.

Mum chose to have her ashes scattered on Primrose Hill, a ten-minute walk from our house and one of her favorite places. We're going to do that next week, just Imogen, Dad, Gran, and me. From the very top, you can see all of London spread out in front of you like a picnic blanket. Before Imogen was born, Mum and Dad used to go there on dates, and when we were little, they'd take us to the top of the hill in our strollers and point out all the sights, like the London Eye and the Shard. We would sled there in the winter and fly kites there on windy autumn days. When I was about five, I rode my scooter down the hill. I was going too fast and fell off at the bottom into a pile of dog poo. Imogen laughed all the way home while I cried. Mum carried me and got dog poo on her dress, but she didn't seem to mind. Apart from that, Primrose Hill is one of my favorite places too.

There is a big piece of stone at the top of the hill with these words by a poet named William Blake engraved on it: "I have conversed with the spiritual Sun. I saw him on Primrose Hill."

It's where I will look for her.

Kate and I head over to Gran. She's sitting at a corner table, deep in conversation with the vicar, who's holding her hand between both of his. I hadn't thought about how Gran must be feeling today. She is Mum's mum and not just my gran. It seems stupid to only be realizing that now. How awful for her to have lost her only child. The lump in my throat that's been there all day seems to grow. I struggle to swallow as I stand in front of her.

"Hello, Kitty, my darling," Gran says and holds out her arms. I climb onto her lap even though I'm really too big now and slump into her. She rests her cheek gently against my head, and we sit there quietly. I suddenly feel exhausted and wish I could go to sleep.

"This room is quite lovely," says the vicar, his booming voice interrupting the quiet. Why do people always feel the need to fill silent spaces with words? Maybe the vicar thinks it's part of his duties to keep the conversation flowing.

We all look politely around the airy space, the gray

light washing in through the windows. I would bet five pounds that the walls are painted with Farrow & Ball number 274, Ammonite, named after the color of fossils like the ones we found on holiday in Dorset last summer. Kate smiles at me and mouths the word Ammonite. She's the one who introduced me to the wonderful world of paint colors. I give her a small nod in return, but I can't find a smile to give back to her.

"It is lovely," says Gran. "You would never even know you were in a pub."

Gran thought it was inappropriate to hold the postfuneral gathering in a pub, "gastro or not," but Dad had calmly ticked off the practicalities of the venue on his hand.

"It's close to the church, our house is too small, and I'm pretty sure you don't want to host it at your place, Eleanor, as some of Laura's patients will be there. Do you really want half a dozen kids running around your living room?"

Dad was right about the children—many of Mum's regular patients are here, along with their parents, her university friends, colleagues from the clinic, neighbors, and even a few of our teachers, who must have taken the day off school to be there. I was astonished to see Miss Barton outside the church. I always thought Mum had driven her crazy by regularly sharing her child-psychology wisdom during parents' evenings, but apparently not, since my teary-eyed English teacher hugged me and told me how wonderful she thought Mum was.

"I quite agree, Eleanor," replies the vicar. "I may recommend this location to other families. It strikes me that this room would work equally well for a christening party or even a small wedding reception, and the food is absolutely delicious!"

The vicar's plate is piled precariously high with a tower of mini Yorkshire puddings, Scotch eggs, small sausage rolls, and little triangles of Welsh rarebit, all of which were Mum's favorite comfort foods.

"Do you know, when Laura was a child, she thought that Welsh rarebit was made from Welsh rabbits? I had to explain to her that it was just a name for posh cheese on toast, but she didn't believe me for years. She flat-out refused to eat it until she was about seven, and cried when anyone else did. Her favorite book was *Peter Rabbit* at the time." Gran smiles at the memory. "Would you like anything to eat, Kitty, dear?"

"No, thank you. I'm not hungry," I say.

The vicar looks embarrassed by his healthy appetite, and edges his overflowing plate to the side of the table.

"Oh, for heaven's sake!" Gran says. "Can you believe it? Sorry, Vicar, but Mrs. Allison has brought that damned dog with her."

We all turn to the door and see our neighbor bustling in with Sir Lancelot, her asthmatic French bulldog, in her arms. Sir Lancelot is a glum-looking creature, constantly snuffling and with numerous digestive issues resulting in horrible farts, which Dad says cause flowers to wilt. In our three years of living next door to Mrs. Allison, she had always been very friendly, but we never got to know her well, busy as we were with life. However, when the shadow of death appeared, so did Mrs. Allison, and over the next six months, she'd become a regular visitor to our house. She popped around almost daily with casseroles, banana bread, and apple tarts, the ubiquitous Sir Lancelot panting placidly at her heels. Dad and Gran found her visits annoying, and I even overheard Gran describe Mrs. Allison as an ambulance chaser, but Mum was very fond of her, and everyone enjoyed her cooking. I think Mum felt that in Mrs. Allison, she had recruited another valuable member for "Team Wentworth"—one who would ensure that we ate well when Mum was no longer in the kitchen. Gran eats like a bird—a slice of bread, some hard cheese, and an apple are her go-to supper. Dad is a big fan of takeout curries and frozen pizza. Mrs. Allison, however, is a talented and prolific baker of pies, stews, tarts, and pastries.

"Hello, all!" says Mrs. Allison, her indigo hat quivering

along with her bottom lip. She sets Sir Lancelot down on the floor next to the vicar with relief. I know from experience that dog is heavy.

"Beautiful service, wasn't it? Just lovely. And the choir—well, music always gets me right here." Mrs. Allison presses her ample bosom mournfully. "Stop it, Sir Lancelot! I'm so sorry, Vicar. I think he's after your Yorkshire pudding."

Sir Lancelot is wheezing even more than usual, his eyes bulging out of his small, round head. Even Gran looks concerned.

"Poor baby, are you hungry? Did mummy not give you enough breakfast?" Mrs. Allison asks the dog, reaching down to pat him. In response, Sir Lancelot makes a surprisingly agile leap toward the vicar's plate and manages to grab a sausage roll before spilling the rest of the food onto the vicar's lap.

"Oh my!" yelps the vicar, jumping to his feet, which gives Sir Lancelot the opportunity to snaffle a Scotch egg.

"Get down, Sir Lancelot, you naughty boy! I can't take you anywhere."

Mrs. Allison kneels to pick up the food that's on the floor and attempts unsuccessfully to pry the Scotch egg from Sir Lancelot's determined jaws. Gran looks on in horror at the vicar, who is trying in vain to wipe the gloopy melted cheese of the Welsh rarebit from his black trousers.

I catch Kate's eye and smile for what feels like the first time in weeks.

"I really hope that your mum saw that," Kate whispers in my ear. "She would have absolutely loved the look on your gran's face."

CHAPTER FOUR

BACK TO SCHOOL

We are going back to school today, which everyone agrees is by far the best place for us to be. Imogen has been flitting about the house ever since the funeral. She walks into rooms, then spins around and leaves. She switches television channels manically and opens and closes books without reading a single word. She looks in the fridge and shuts it again without taking anything out. The energy radiates off her, in stark contrast to my lethargy. I drag myself between my bedroom, the bathroom, and the kitchen. I avoid the living room, which is flooded with light and air, since Gran has taken to leaving the doors open to let the outside in. I find the garden offensive. It's bustling with life as flowers burst into color, and birds hop around the lawn, watched by my cat, Cleo, who skulks in the bushes. All I want to do is sleep, but Dad or Gran, one of whom comes into my room every day before I'm even awake, coaxes me out of bed each morning before eight. Sleeping is the only escape. The horrible part is waking up, because, for a few moments, I struggle to figure out what is wrong before the realization washes over me, taking my breath away. One morning I forgot that Mum was dead for about twenty seconds, and then it hit me. I was crushed under a ton of rocks of sadness. These days one or all of us emerge from our separate bedrooms in the morning looking as if we've just crawled out of a collapsed building, invisible dust covering us and pain pressing on our chests.

I don't dream, I never have, well, not that I can remember. Imogen does though, and sometimes I hear her crying out in her sleep. I go to her room and often, Dad is already there, stroking her hair. If he's not, I sit down and do it until she settles. I like doing that for her. A few years ago in our old house, where Imogen and I shared a room, she woke up in the night screaming that praying mantises were climbing up her bed. I had no idea what a praying mantis was, but it sounded terrifying, so I raced to Mum and Dad's room, my shrieks even louder than my sister's. My parents were both already out of bed and running down the landing toward our room. Mum scooped me up in her arms while Dad charged into the bedroom to face Imogen's demons. Later, when Imogen and I had been calmed down with cuddles and cups of warm milk and were tucked back into our mantis-free beds, I told my sister that she should keep garlic under her pillow from now on.

"What for?" she asked suspiciously.

"The praying mantis, of course. They don't like garlic or daylight."

"Kitty, you idiot. They're a type of insect, not vampires!"

I could tell by her voice that she was smiling, and that made me feel happy. The next day I stole two cloves of garlic from the kitchen and tucked one under each of our mattresses, and guess what—no more praying mantises.

It feels strange to walk through the familiar school gates. Mrs. Brooks, our scarily efficient headmistress, is standing by the front door as she does every day, shaking hands with each girl, ensuring they make eye contact while they do so and giving them a top-to-toe sweep of her steely eyes as she checks for uniform violations. In my first year at the school, Mrs. Brooks had told Mum that the glossy, black patent leather shoes I was proudly sporting were more suitable for parties than for the classroom. Mum returned her steady gaze, and politely explained that these were the shoes I would be wearing until my feet grew out of them, but that she would be sure to buy plain leather next time.

As Imogen and I file through the door, the headmistress embraces us. She looks bony and angular but is surprisingly soft to touch.

"Welcome back, girls. I want you to know that the whole community at Haverstock Girls' School is here to support you during this difficult time. You may come and see me whenever you feel the need to talk. I have a kettle in my office and a rather large supply of excellent chocolate chip cookies." She smiles, and her eyes crinkle in a friendly way. "Even if you would simply like to sit quietly, read a book, and have a cookie, you will be very welcome."

Mrs. Brooks considers Imogen's eyeliner and non-uniform-compliant black tights—they should be navy—but apparently decides to give her a pass on her first day back since she gently herds us through the glossy red doors.

"Are you going to go and have a chocolate chip cookie with Mrs. Brooks, Imo?" I ask.

"God, no! She won't let you just sit there and read, you know. You'll have to talk to her about your feelings."

Imogen disappears into a gaggle of navy-blue girls, and I watch her go, feeling lost. I'd like to have a cookie and a cup of tea in Mrs. Brooks's office. It's always lovely and quiet up there, just the friendly ticktocking of the grandmother clock.

"Well, it is a girls' school after all, Kitty, dear," Mrs. Brooks said when I told her that I liked the grandfather clock.

Jessica greets me with a hug and proceeds to stay doggedly by my side for the rest of the day, her arm looped protectively through mine. She only unhooks her arm during lessons, while we eat lunch, and when one of us goes to the loo. Jess doesn't ask about the funeral but just says that her mum said it was "beautiful" and then pauses to see if I want to say anything. When I don't reply, she starts to tell me about a family of foxes that has recently taken up residence underneath her garden shed. Jess loves all animals and wants to be a vet or a wildlife television presenter when she grows up—probably both if she has time. She's been trying to lure the foxes out from under the shed with various types of food stolen from her kitchen.

"I left a sandwich out for them this morning," she says. "They didn't eat the apple slices I left them yesterday, so I cut up a cheddar cheese sandwich into fox-bite-size pieces. It was whole-wheat bread, because my mum won't buy the white stuff. I hope the foxes don't mind. I prefer white bread. Foxes probably do too."

"You could try cat treats," I say, grateful that the conversation has moved on. "I could bring in some of Cleo's tomorrow if the foxes don't like the sandwiches. Or I could ask Mrs. Allison for some of Sir Lancelot's treats."

"Brilliant idea! Why didn't I think of that? I'll call you when I get home to let you know if they ate the sandwiches."

"How will you know that it was the foxes that ate them and not a bird or something?"

"Birds don't eat cheese sandwiches, Kitty," Jess says confidently, so we leave it at that.

Even though there is more to distract me at school than at home, Mum is still everywhere. I know she'd enjoy the book we have just started in English, *The Secret Garden*. I bet she read it when she was younger; I'll ask Gran. Mum could have helped me with my French homework of writing a conversation in a café. "Je voudrais un croissant" is as far as I've got. Who is going to help me with French and English now? My parents divided any homework help that Imogen or I might need between the two of them. Mum always said that she did the words and Dad did the numbers in their relationship.

In art, we're finishing our drawings of the sarcophagus that we sketched when we went on a school trip to the British Museum two weeks ago. Mrs. Kerr, the art teacher, looks mortified when she catches my eye after telling the class to continue to work on their mummies. I give her a sympathetic smile to let her know not to feel awkward about it, and to show her that I'm fine, I walk across the classroom to sharpen my pencils. A memory smacks me right between the eyes of Mum and her automatic pencil sharpener. Dad laughed at her for buying it, but she loved it. I used to sit next to her at the kitchen table handing her one pencil after another, which she stuck into the machine and pushed down, causing it to whirr until a little click indicated that the pencil was ready. Mum would remove it and study its perfect point with satisfaction. My job was to empty the curly shavings when the sharpener was full. Mum said they would have made excellent bedding for a hamster if we had one. Dad muttered something about lead poisoning, and then I delivered ten perfectly sharpened pencils to Imogen. All of this comes back to me as I stand frozen in the classroom, my unsharpened pencil in hand. It's like I'm in an episode of *Doctor Who* and entered the Tardis only to emerge five years earlier in my kitchen with Mum's warm arm resting against mine.

Gran is waiting for us at the school gates at the end of the day.

"I know, girls, I know, you're old enough to walk home

by yourselves, but I just happened to be passing, and I thought that we could all go and get a smoothie."

"I have an appointment with Anna, don't forget," says Imogen.

"How about you, Kitty?" says Gran, taking my hand. "You don't see Sam today, do you?"

"No, but I'd like to go straight home please."

Imogen and I are seeing different counselors from mum's old practice twice a week, and have been doing so for the last six weeks. Imogen sees Anna, and I see Sam. Sam gave me a copy of *The Child's Guide to Losing a Parent*, which says that I may be about to enter the rage stage. I'm quite looking forward to it. Having license to smash plates, scream, shout, and be rude to people while they have to "give me space to grieve" sounds most satisfying. I can clearly see in my mind a red-faced howling girl grabbing crockery from the shelves and hurling it across the room. I would reach first for the fancy floral china plates covered in pale-pink and deep-blue flowers with a gilt rim. They're antiques and not allowed to go in the dishwasher, so have to be ever so carefully washed up, which is annoying. However, instead of the energetic, spiky rage I long for, I feel utterly exhausted, like a wrung-out dish towel. I wish I never had to speak again, or wash my hair, or eat, all of which seem to take monumental effort. It's like when I had the flu last year.

For days and weeks afterward, I felt floppy and feeble, needing to sit down at the top of the stairs whenever I went up to my bedroom.

Sam told me in one of our early sessions, when Mum was still alive, that he considers himself to be a companion to me in my pain. That he is there to bear witness to it without trying to take it away or to protect me from the truth of what will be lost. The last time I visited Sam, he asked me why I tell people that Mum had breast cancer instead of lung cancer.

"Does it make a difference to you, Kitty, what type of cancer your mum had, I mean?"

"Yes, it does, actually."

"Why?"

"When I tell people that Mum had lung cancer, they ask me if she smoked, like it matters. When I say that she never did, they look surprised and say, what bad luck, as if otherwise it was partly her fault."

Sam sat listening and nodded for me to continue. He often does this. Mum once told me that the more the patient talks, the better the therapist. Sam uses his words prudently. Anyone would think he was charged ten pounds each time he uttered a sentence.

"So, now I just say cancer. If people ask me what type I say breast cancer, which seems the most appropriate kind for a mother to have. Also, everyone seems to know someone who's had breast cancer, so they start telling me about a half-marathon they're running to raise money or show me one of those pink ribbons pinned to their jackets. It's the best way to change the subject."

"I understand," Sam said. "You do know that you don't have to answer questions about your mum being ill, right? It's fine to say you don't want to talk about it, even to me, and it's my job."

"Well, guess what Gran told me. She said that about one hundred people die of lung cancer in this country every single day, and fifteen of them have never smoked."

Gran had turned to the internet when Mum was diagnosed to learn everything she could about treatments until it became clear that for her girl, there was no cure. Then she turned her energy to raising money and awareness. The inequitable funding of lung-cancer research became her specialized subject.

"Lung cancer is known as the poor cousin among cancers. A paltry seven hundred and eight pounds is spent on lung-cancer research for every person who dies from it, compared to three thousand five hundred pounds for breast cancer and a whopping ten thousand pounds for testicular cancer. It's an outrage," Gran said to anyone who would listen.

She insisted on including these facts in the newspaper notice about Mum's death and wanted to put it at the back of the order of service for the funeral, but Mum said no.

"We need to fund research for all types of cancer, Mum," she said, "not just lung cancer. It isn't a competition between illnesses."

But Gran was on a mission to raise the profile of the poor relative among cancers. That particular cancer, the one that stole her only child from her, became her sworn enemy. Mum asked that flowers not be sent to the funeral and instead for people to make a donation to Cancer Research UK or the Marie Curie hospice, where she spent her last two weeks. Some people still sent huge bouquets of suffocatingly scented flowers both to the church and to our house. Dad said they probably also gave money, but Gran and I both thought it was silly of them, and they should have just added whatever they spent on flowers to the donation. Gran scares lots of people, but cancer wafted her away like an annoying fly. Nobody and nothing could defeat it.

"Talking does help, you know, Kitty," says Sam, bringing me back to the small, overheated office and his concerned gaze.

He would say that, otherwise he'd be out of a job.

CHAPTER FIVE

PONYTAIL GIRL TO THE RESCUE

Grief permeates our house, drifting into every corner like the fog that sometimes swallows up Hampstead Heath. I watch as if from above as it reaches into the heart of each member of my family.

It weighs Dad down—his center of gravity seems to have shifted, and his mouth, shoulders, head, and hands are all pulled toward the ground.

Imogen's strange restlessness continues. She jumps at unexpected sounds, tosses and turns at night, clenches her teeth, and constantly taps her right foot. Skittish, Gran calls it, and says that Imogen is like an agitated racehorse prancing sideways at the starting line, waiting for the gun.

Gran herself seems oddly absent. Her gaze drifts off into the distance and when I say her name she looks surprised to see me, blinking vacantly. Gran was always so utterly present before Mum died that the change in her is more unsettling than Dad's or Imogen's behavior. I find myself holding on to Gran when I'm with her, demanding her attention like a toddler, trying to tether her to me instead of letting her drift off into her memories.

Kate, like Imogen, is a ball of energy. She bounces around on her visits, touching and hugging all of us and bestowing lip balms, hair ties, bath bombs, and cute pastel notebooks embossed with things like Reach for the Stars, Follow Your Dreams, and Look for the Magic, which pile up on my desk, their pages unmarked.

Cleo mews mournfully outside Mum and Dad's bedroom door, which is closed to her since she stopped using her litter box and started peeing on their bed, her own silent protest to her favorite person's unexplained absence.

Only Mrs. Allison appears immune to the miasma, baking up a storm in our kitchen to blow it away with sugar, frosting, and whipped cream.

I'm always cold these days and bundle myself up in cardigans and scarves from Mum's wardrobe. Despite the sunny April days, my nails have a bluish tinge to them. I lie on my bed and look around my room in awe at the evidence of the energetic and productive life I used to lead. There are photographs of Jess and me climbing trees, drawings of Cleo in various poses, an unfinished scarf from when Mum tried to teach me how to knit, my beloved paint charts including my own color creations, medals for swimming, certificates from school, homemade vases, and a box I made covered in shells. And everywhere I look, there are photos of Mum. Mum at home, on holiday, swimming in the sea, horse riding, hugging us, on a bike, eating breakfast, reading, giving me a piggyback ride, making a snowman, smiling, smiling, smiling—so many moments captured, but no more to be made.

Life does go on though, and this is apparently our new normal. How to survive the unsurvivable? You just do. Gran told me that the prime minister in the Second World War, Winston Churchill, said: "When you are going through hell, keep going." He was quite right, and we get up every morning, even if we don't want to, and we go down to the kitchen and eat breakfast. Imogen pushes cereal around her bowl while Dad watches her. I munch toast and Marmite and watch them both. We go to school and to work. We talk to people, answer questions, smile when needed, even laugh sometimes, eat at the appropriate times, come home, go to bed, and then do it all over again. Sam says that routine is healing, but I think it's basic survival.

* * *

At some point over the next few weeks, Imogen goes back to ignoring me at school. When Mum was very ill, Imogen started talking to me during the day, even coming to sit with me at lunch sometimes and walking to and from school next to me instead of ten steps ahead. It's strangely comforting to go back to our standard social operating model. Jessica, on the other hand, still never leaves my side. She's like a loyal golden retriever, always there, ready to play or sit quietly. She positively growls at anyone who might upset me. Her protectiveness is sweet, but stifling. I felt disloyal when I said to Sam that Jess sometimes gets on my nerves and I wish we could go back to the way we were before.

Jess and I are sitting in the playground on one of the few benches, attempting to do our French homework, when Scarlett Wilson and a couple of her friends saunter over, their identical ponytails swinging with self-importance. How do they get them to swing in the same direction like that? My hair will barely go into a ponytail, and Jess has curly hair, which doesn't really swing, but springs around wildly. The idea of Jess and I being able to synchronize the movements of our hair is laughable—an unattainable goal for us mere mortals. Scarlett is in the year above Imogen and is the self-appointed queen of the school although I think she looks a bit like a weasel.

"Move, you two! Senior school privileges," they chorus in identical bored voices.

Usually that would be enough to get us off the bench, but today I don't feel like moving and Jess, after giving me an anxious sideways glance, is along for the ride.

"No," I say. "We're not moving. You move."

Scarlett scowls at me.

"Oh, I'm so sorry, I forgot you get dead-mum privileges. How long do they last, by the way? How long do we have to be nice to the Wentworth sisters? Your mum had lung cancer, didn't she? Maybe she shouldn't have smoked!"

I jump to my feet, my face blazing, but before I can spit out a reply, Imogen descends from nowhere like an avenging angel.

"Scarlett Wilson, you are such a pathetic bitch," Imogen says. She speaks softly and enunciates each syllable, the quietness of her voice adding weight and menace to her words. "My sister will sit exactly where she wants to sit. In fact, I think I'll sit here with her."

Imogen plonks herself down, pulling me back onto the bench, and picks up my dog-eared French textbook, which she starts leafing through.

"Oh, I remember studying this," she says, addressing

Jess and me as if Scarlett and her friends don't exist. "It was so easy!"

Imogen looks up at Scarlett and her friends and acts all surprised to see them still standing there.

"Oh, wow, you're still here. You can go now, but thanks so much for coming."

Jess and I look on in amazement as the group of girls storms back across the playground. As soon as they're out of sight, Imogen shoves the book at me, rolls her eyes, and strolls off.

"Wow!" says Jess. "That was cool."

"It was," I say, watching my sister disappear across the playground. Her own ponytail, the glossiest of them all, looks like a superhero's secret weapon. This would make a good book, I decide—*Ponytail Girl*, watch her save the world, and then make a YouTube video for a homemade deep-conditioning avocado hair treatment. The bell rings, and Jess and I troop in for our English lesson. I spend the rest of the afternoon writing notes and designing a stylish costume for Ponytail Girl with a range of coordinating scrunchies she can shoot off her wrists. The ponytail can extend or contract as needed, and Ponytail Girl can use it like Spider-Man uses his web shooters to swing from building to building. I think to maximize the dramatic impact of the ponytail, our heroine should be able to jettison it, like a lizard losing its tail, except cooler. The ponytail can then be used either as chains to imprison villains or as a detachable whip to fight the forces of evil. In its place, a new, even more lustrous ponytail would grow instantly. This character has a lot of potential.

CHAPTER SIX

EAVESDROPPING

Mrs. Allison has taken up residence in our kitchen. Most afternoons, when I get home from school, she's there, up to her elbows in flour, Sir Lancelot panting under the kitchen table. Her baking is fantastic. Tins of gooey marmalade cake, glossy lemon tarts, and fluffy chocolate chip muffins are piled up in the cupboards. Mrs. Allison has just found out that she has a place as a contestant on the latest season of *The Great British Bake Off*, and when she isn't baking, she is reading recipe books and rewatching episodes from previous seasons. Unfortunately, Mrs. Allison spending so much time at our house has not improved her relationship with Gran, who is constantly complaining about her to Dad.

"Elizabeth is such a busybody. Doesn't she realize that we have quite enough to cope with without her taking over the kitchen and ruining the girls' appetites with her sugar-laden concoctions? I'm sure that dog shouldn't be slobbering around when she's baking. Most unhygienic."

Our appetites are their battleground. As Gran tries to fill us up with sugar-free and salt-free lentil soups and casseroles, Mrs. Allison retaliates with yummy Swedish cinnamon buns and Italian cream-filled rolls called cannoli. In a concession to healthy eating, she made carrot cake, but Gran, having looked up the recipe, found it contained four hundred grams of sugar.

"Half of it was brown sugar," Mrs. Allison protested.

Dad describes being stuck in the middle of Gran and Mrs. Allison's culinary hostilities as being "caught between a rock and a hard place." At least that's what he told Dominic earlier this week when he came over to our house for supper. I haven't lost the habit of listening at doors that I developed when Mum got sick. It's the only way I have of finding out how Dad really feels.

"I can't believe I'm a widower," he said. "Did you know that if a widower remarries, he's not called a widower anymore? How can that make sense?"

"Do you think you ever would?" asked Dominic.

I nearly fell through the door as I strained to hear Dad's reply.

"God, I don't know, Dom. I can't imagine it, but I can't imagine being on my own for the rest of my life either.

What am I going to do when the girls have gone off to university? Hang out here with Eleanor, Mrs. Allison, and the cat?"

"Don't forget the dog. You'll have Sir Lancelot for male bonding."

Without waiting to hear another word, I raced upstairs to Imogen's room.

"Kitty, how many times have I told you to knock before you barge in here? Get out!"

"Dad says he's going to get married again! He just told Dominic."

"What? When?"

"I heard them talking just now. Dad said he'll get married, so he doesn't have to live here with Gran and Mrs. Allison when we've gone to university." I burst into angry tears.

Imogen grabbed me by the hand, swirled me down the stairs, and we hurtled into the kitchen.

"Did you just say you'd get married again? Mum only died ten weeks ago. It's disgusting!" she said.

"Girls, girls, calm down!" Dad held his hands up as if he was trying to tame a pair of wild ponies. "Imogen, what on earth are you talking about?"

"Kitty heard you. She was listening at the kitchen door just now."

"Kitty, love, you really have to stop listening at doors,"

Dad sighed. "We've talked about this before. It can cause all sorts of misunderstandings and hurt feelings. Yes, Dominic did ask me if I might ever get married again, and I told him that I couldn't imagine it, but I also can't envisage myself being on my own for the rest of my life. I miss your mum every single minute of every day."

I broke free of Imogen and ran to Dad. Imogen joined us in a family hug, while Dominic stood looking awkward, probably wishing he could disappear. I think he blamed himself for the drama. Imogen and I left the kitchen, but while my sister headed straight back to her room, I lingered in the hallway.

"For God's sake," said Dad. "What am I supposed to tell them, Dom? That I feel absolutely lost without Laura? That the world doesn't make sense without her? That I love them more than life itself and that if the three of us can just hold on to each other, we'll be okay?"

"That last one sounds good to me, mate."

"I sometimes think the girls wish," Dad continued in a shaky voice, "I mean, I know they do, they wish they still had their mum, and that it was me who had died. It would have been easier for everyone."

"No, Rob! You mustn't ever think that. The girls love you. They love you and Laura. They don't want you *or* her. They want both of you."

I slipped away in shame, wishing I could unhear what Dad had just said.

Still, I can't get the idea of Dad getting married again out of my head, so after overhearing that conversation, I start checking Dad's laptop for signs of him visiting dating websites or other suspicious online activity. This isn't as bad as it sounds because I am allowed to use his computer. He even gave me his username and password so I could log on if I needed to when he isn't here. I'm only really supposed to use the laptop for homework, though, so to make me feel less guilty, I do my online sleuthing when I've finished my homework.

This evening I have to research life in Viking Britain as part of my history assignment. We're going on a school trip to the Viking Center in York next week. Imogen went three years ago and said it's "dullsville," but I'm looking forward to it. The museum has life-size dioramas depicting everyday scenes from Viking Britain. I'm writing the diary of a Viking girl for the main part of my project. I named her Alfhild, which translates to "battle of the elves." What a cool name! Vikings have a terrible reputation, but they weren't all bloodthirsty marauders. Alfhild and her family live peacefully on a farm, which does make for some quite dull diary entries.

I gave Alfhild a kind older brother named Ingolf, who is much nicer than my non-Viking sister with the same initial. He has a pet wolf and a more fun life than Alfhild's, because he gets to look after the animals while she's stuck in the longhouse making stew and sweeping the hearth.

When I've finished writing today's entry, an unusually exciting day for Alfhild since some of the sheep have escaped into the longhouse and trashed it, Imogen and I get to work on Dad's laptop. She shows me how to look through the history of websites that Dad has visited. Top of the list is a site called Flying Solo, which apparently offers support for parents "going it alone after the death of a partner." Dad's username on the forum is WWLD, which he explains in his introductory post stands for "What Would Laura Do?"

"Laura was my wife's name," he wrote, "and I think WWLD about a hundred times a day as I do my best to raise our two daughters."

There was a flurry of welcoming replies from other community members who have names like Emma1982, Snoopy, MrB, Fairydust, and JDNYC. I find the comments fascinating, and the website has a helpful feature that stores the logged-in member's posts in a separate tab so that we can easily check all of Dad's comments and questions. His most recent post was:

"How often should I talk to the girls about their mum? I want to keep the memory of her alive, but I don't want to make it seem contrived or morbid. Sometimes when I mention her, the girls look upset and clam up. Any advice would be appreciated. TIA, WWLD."

The responses are mostly sensible.

"WWLD, you should talk about your wife as often as feels natural to you."

"Take your cues from your kids. Why not ask them what they think?"

"I'm sure you are doing an amazing job. Be kind to yourself."

A few are bizarre: one, in particular, causes Imogen and me to pause in our scrolling:

"I always find myself speaking to my husband as if he were still with us. I'm not sure what my kids think, but it feels right to me."

"I can imagine what her kids think," says Imogen. "They think—'Oh crap, our dad's dead and our mum has completely lost her mind!' Some of these people are total weirdos. Dad might actually be doing a good job of 'Flying Solo' after all. What a cheesy name for a website."

One response makes me feel terrible.

"D's dad died before he was born and I'm sure I talk about him way too much. D seems to love hearing stories about his dad, but he's only four. I'll see how it goes as he gets older. Good luck. JDNYC."

The awfulness of never having known your mum or dad is too much to comprehend. At least I had ten years of having a mum and a dad.

I could have continued reading the posts for hours, but Imogen says it's getting boring and shuts down the laptop. As soon as she leaves the room, I log back on and quickly write another entry in Alfhild's diary. Ingolf falls into the stream, catches a cold, and is subsequently bedridden. Alfhild has to take over his animal care duties for the next few days until he has recovered, which is quite a relief since there are only so many times I can write about the poor girl sweeping the floor and sewing mittens. After finishing this gripping and most satisfying diary entry, I go back to the Flying Solo home page and sign up for my own account. I ignore all the disclaimers, cheerfully clicking the boxes agreeing that I am over eighteen, etc., and within minutes have my own profile set up under the username MMM for Miss My Mum. I am going to have some excellent advice for WWLD. For example, he should under no circumstances consider getting into a romantic relationship, and the younger child in a family should always get more attention than the older sibling, who was lucky enough to have priceless additional years with his or her parent.

✳ ✳ ✳

I don't tell Sam about the website Flying Solo. He's always giving me books to read about grief with titles like *Healing your Heart* and *Love and Loss for Tweens*. He gave me a journal to record my "grief journey," as he called it. Sam also recommended local support groups and even told Dad about a club for kids who've lost a parent. Imogen and I refused to go. Come to think of it, Sam probably already knows about Flying Solo. He may even be the one who told Dad about it. There's a strong possibility Sam would recognize me as MMM, so I'll have to be careful to disguise myself. I do ask Sam things though—things that I can't talk to anyone else about, things that keep me awake at night.

"Do you think Mum was scared?"

"Scared of what, Kitty?" Sam says, even though I'm 100 percent sure he knows exactly what I'm talking about. He just wants me to say the words.

"Scared of dying."

If Sam asks me if I think Mum was frightened I might punch him in the face. He does this sometimes, turns the question back on me, which is another classic therapist technique that Mum used on us all the time at home. He doesn't throw it back at me though but looks at me thoughtfully.

"Laura used to talk a lot about how much she was going to miss you, Imogen, and your dad. She talked about how proud she was of all of you, but your mum never told me she was scared. That doesn't mean she wasn't frightened though."

"I would be scared and furious. Why wasn't Mum angrier, Sam? Gran's the only one apart from me who gets mad about it. Sometimes when Gran talks about the cancer, I see her clench her fists until her knuckles turn white."

"Have you ever talked to your gran about feeling angry? Maybe you should, Kitty. It might help her to know she's not the only one white-knuckling it."

"Maybe," I say, knowing that I won't. I don't need to. Gran sees my rage as clearly as I see hers. We don't need to talk about it. She knows. Our hands are clenched in fists of fury right next to each other. She also sees how scared I am. No one ever told me that grief feels like fear and that I'd be terrified every single day.

"Anything else, Kitty?" Sam asks, using his mind-reading techniques.

"Nothing important," I tell him, but even as I say it, I know I won't be able to hold it in much longer.

CHAPTER SEVEN

KNEADING THERAPY

As the days pass, I get more scared, not less. I jolt awake with my heart racing and my mouth dry. My eyes shoot open, and I scan the room for hidden terrors. I feel wide, wide awake. I'm afraid of growing up without my mum. I'm terrified that something terrible is going to happen to Dad, Imogen, Gran, Kate, Jess, or Cleo. I'm scared that my love will have nowhere to go. I'm afraid to read Mum's birthday letter. I decide to focus my fears on the letter, which is the only one I have any control over, since I could choose to tuck it away until I'm not afraid anymore. Last night I lay awake thinking about it—I imagined opening the envelope and it containing a blank sheet of paper, or maybe worse, words from Mum that don't sound like her or that tell me something I don't want to know.

As well as having Sam to talk to, Mrs. Allison acts as

my unofficial, unpaid, and unqualified therapist. Today when I get home, she is already in the kitchen laying out ingredients, bowls, wooden spoons, spatulas, and baking trays.

"Hello, dear," she says when I walk in and slump down at the table, dark circles under my eyes. "Oh no, not a good day at school?"

"Not really."

"Well, why don't you make some bread with me? Pounding away at dough is as good a way to get rid of stress as I've ever found. Some people say that bread tastes best when it's made with love, but the most wonderful loaf I ever baked was the one I made after I found out about William and that floozy from his office. Do you know what he said to me when I confronted him about his affair? 'The heart wants what it wants, Lizzie.' How dare he quote Emily bloody Dickinson to me? I'll tell you something else Emily Dickinson said, she said, 'a wounded deer leaps highest.' Well, she was right, wasn't she, as here I am, all cozy in Belsize Park with you and Sir Lancelot, and about to be a television star, and last I heard William was living in a nasty apartment in Clacton-on-Sea with soon-to-be wife number three."

Mrs. Allison had kicked out her husband, "the Lothario of North London," as Dad calls him, after she found out about his latest dalliance. This was many years before we moved in, so we never got to meet him. Even though he sounds like a complete loser, Mrs. Allison says he is the only man she could ever love, which is why Sir Lancelot is now her chosen life partner.

"Now, let's get on with it. We're going to bake an eight-strand plaited loaf. It was the technical challenge on *Bake Off* last season, so we're not likely to get it again, but you never know. Those judges can be tricky. Grab an apron, Kitty. You're going to make one all by yourself."

Two hours later, my navy uniform covered in flour, I am feeling better. I had battered my dough relentlessly, but my loaf didn't rise well. It looks as if it's been sat on in the oven, while Mrs. Allison's bread is so gloriously plump that you could use it as a pillow. Mrs. Allison said I overworked the dough, but since I seemed to be finding it therapeutic she'd decided to leave me to it. I was good at plaiting the strands of dough though; all those hours of braiding my dolls' hair had set me up well for that part of the recipe. Over a cup of hot chocolate and a slice of Mrs. Allison's loaf with some of her homemade blackberry jam, I unburden myself about the letters. I keep my other fears to myself. They're just too big to talk about to anyone.

"What if Mum doesn't sound like herself? She knew everything about me from the time I was born, but she doesn't know me now. She wrote those letters to an imaginary future Kitty, one who's probably much nicer than me. She always thought I was a better person than I am."

"Oh, I think your mum knew exactly who you are, Kitty Wentworth, and that is an absolutely lovely girl who is growing up to be a wonderful young lady. It's a great sadness to me that Mr. Allison and I were never able to have a family, although given his shortcomings maybe that was a blessing. I do know a thing or two about mothers though, and mine always used to say that the very first time she looked into my eyes, she knew precisely who I was. It was the same with Laura—she knew you inside and out, Kitty."

Mrs. Allison pats my hand and wipes away the tears that I hadn't noticed falling down my cheeks with the corner of her floury apron.

"Right then, madam, next up, sticky toffee pudding."

"I think I'll just watch you if that's okay," I say. Despite her lack of qualifications, Mrs. Allison is quite a good therapist. She talks a lot more than Sam though.

"That's fine. We can pretend you're one of the judges. I need to get used to an audience. Do you know that as well as the other contestants, presenters, and judges, there'll be camera people, directors, producers, and heavens knows who else in the tent? Do you think they'll have someone to do my hair and makeup?"

Filming starts soon for Mrs. Allison's season of *The Great British Bake Off*. She's been trying to lose weight in preparation for her television appearance.

"They say the camera adds ten pounds, Kitty, so I decided if I lose ten then I'll look exactly like myself."

In the competing priorities of a slimmed-down waistline and needing to taste her biscuits, cakes, and puddings in order to perfect them, baking is the hands-down winner.

"You don't need to lose any weight, Lizzie," Dad told her last week. "What's that old saying? Never trust a skinny baker."

That weekend, Mrs. Allison persuades me to go shopping with her to buy new outfits for the show. She chooses ten brightly colored, short-sleeved linen shirts in shades that Farrow & Ball will likely never make into paints. The changing room is an explosion of lime green, shocking pink, lurid orange, a vibrant shade of aqua, and electric blue. She also selects three pairs of comfortable khaki trousers and two pairs of white capris. The capris are not particularly flattering, but Mrs. Allison possesses what Mum would have described as a refreshingly healthy body image along with an extra serving of self-confidence. She maintains a cheerful running commentary through the curtain of the changing room.

"These trousers are perfect because they've got a bit of stretch in them, which I'll need for bending down to get things in and out of the oven."

The curtains burst open as she does a few daring test lunges in the trousers, much to the surprise of the woman coming out of the neighboring changing room.

"Short-sleeved shirts are so practical for baking since you don't want to keep having to roll your sleeves up, do you? Now, the notes from the producer said no stripes, not that I would wear them anyway, the vertical ones make me look like a deck chair, and the horizontal ones obviously wouldn't work with my chest! They suggest no patterns at all, which is a real shame as there was that lovely floral blouse. Do you know we have to wear the same clothes for both days of filming? I always used to wonder why contestants had the same outfits on the second day—it's for something called continuity. I suppose people wash their clothes overnight, but I don't fancy that so I'm splurging on two of each. I'll leave the tags on in case I can return one of them. I don't want to jinx myself, but I'm buying an outfit for the final."

Mrs. Allison has barely taken a breath during this stream of consciousness. Dad says that she could talk for England. She emerges from the changing room redfaced and triumphant. After we've finished paying for her outfits, Mrs. Allison announces in a loud voice that our next stop is the lingerie department. She pronounces lingerie with a French accent.

"Kitty, I talked to your dad and told him I thought it was time we got you a bra." She looks down at my flat-as-a-pancake chest. "There's not much going on at the moment, but it's essential to have a supportive bra while things are developing. Anyway, he didn't seem keen to discuss it but did agree that I could bring you shopping. You never know, you might suddenly blossom like I did, overnight. By the way, feel free to come to me when you get your period. I know your mum was always very open with you girls about puberty. I'm not a trained professional like her, but I am a graduate of the university of life. If you ever want to ask me anything about periods or whatever, I'm here for you, you know that, don't you, dear? Mind you, it's been a while since I had one!"

She chuckles, and I look around to make sure nobody is listening. Please let her have finished talking about periods and boobs.

Mrs. Allison continues, "M&S is where I got my first bra. It's a British institution, although the queen apparently shops at Rigby & Peller. I went there once, just to have a look, and the bras were a hundred pounds each! Good old M&S charges eighteen pounds. I suppose the queen can afford it, though. Right, I wonder where the smallest bras would be."

"They call them training bras in America," I giggle. "Like your boobs are getting ready for an Olympic event."

"Do they really? The things they say over there. We just call them small. Ah, here they are. Color-wise you can choose from white, cream, or maybe a very pale pink, but nothing too racy. Can you imagine your gran's face if we came home with a red or black bra for you? Look at these, Kitty, the 'Angel First Bra' line, aren't they pretty?"

I pick one up and examine it.

"Can I get padded?"

Mrs. Allison studies my chest.

"How about one padded and one not?" she says. "I used to stuff mine with socks, but not for long. I was an early bloomer. What size do you think? Twenty-eight AA is the smallest, but we should get you measured."

"No way, Mrs. Allison! That would be so embarrassing."

"They've seen it all before, lovey. I read in the Sunday newspaper that eighty percent of women in England are wearing the wrong size bra. You don't want to start off in the wrong size, do you?" Mrs. Allison says this as if the wrong size might lead to ruin, or at the very least to bad posture and saggy boobs.

We look around and locate a lady named Gwen, who tells us she's been working in the underwear department here for nearly forty years, has a grandson studying geography at Durham University, and loves to spend time in her garden. Gwen bustles me into the changing room, measures me in a brisk and businesslike way, and ceremonially pronounces me a twenty-eight A. It's like the sorting hat in Harry Potter placing you in Hufflepuff because to be in Gryffindor you'd need to be a thirty-four B.

"Twenty-eight A!" says Mrs. Allison. "Well done, Kitty! It's not even the smallest size. You'd never think it to look at her, would you, Gwen? Now, let's get these paid for and get back home. I've got profiteroles to make this afternoon. I'm doing a lovely mango crème pâtissière filling for the choux buns with lemon icing on the top, but I'm not sure if I've got the balance of sweet and sour right, so I need you to be my taster please, Kitty."

"I will. Mrs. Allison, please don't tell Imogen or Dad my bra size."

"Of course not. Your secret's safe with me. Just let me know when we need to come back and get the next size up, and we can revisit Gwen."

Mrs. Allison smiles at her new friend, who is excited to tell her colleagues that she just met someone who will be on the upcoming season of her favorite television show.

"The bra ladies from Marks & Spencer will all be

cheering you on, Lizzie. Good luck!"

I take Mrs. Allison's hand as we walk out of the shop. Mum was right; she is an excellent addition to Team Wentworth. I don't know what we'd do without her. I don't know what I'd do without her. We set off down Oxford Street to get the bus home, and I swing the little green carrier bag containing two bras from the 'Angel First Bra' line: one white and one shell pink, both padded! I can't wait to see Mrs. Allison on TV wearing her new outfits, though I do need to find a way to tell her to avoid doing any lunges.

CHAPTER EIGHT

THE GREAT BRITISH BAKER

Filming for *The Great British Bake Off* starts this weekend, and Mrs. Allison is going to an enormous country house called Welford Park in Berkshire where they make the show. I'm in charge of Sir Lancelot while she's away.

"It's the first time we've ever been apart," Mrs. Allison sniffs, burying her face in Sir Lancelot's chubby neck folds as the taxi driver taps his fingers on the steering wheel. "I tried to explain to him that I'll be back on Sunday evening, but I'm not sure he completely understands."

The taxi driver muffles a snort of laughter, and Dad tries to edge Mrs. Allison toward the cab.

"Kitty, I pinned Sir Lancelot's routine up next to the fridge. There's a list of the shops that give him dog treats, so he won't let you get past them without stopping."

"Come on, Mrs. A., you don't want to be late," Dad says as we usher her into the car and wave her off.

"Sir Lancelot says good luck," I shout after the cab as it turns the corner.

"Right, off we go, Kitty," says Gran. "You can bring Sir Lancelot on our fundraising trip. He might even come in useful to encourage dog people to make a donation."

"Let's pin a daffodil on him," I say and take one of the little yellow flower brooches out of Gran's bag and carefully attach it to Sir Lancelot's red collar, making sure he's not going to get the pin stuck in him.

Gran is raising funds for the Marie Curie Hospice, and the daffodil is their symbol. People wear them like poppies to show their support for the charity. Sir Lancelot takes a bit of persuading to get up the hill, and as Mrs. Allison had said, we have to stop at the butcher, the bakery, and the wine shop, where he gets a treat. Gran raises her eyebrows at the wine shop, and I'm surprised the grumpy baker gives out dog treats, but it turns out he also has a French bulldog.

"A bit late for Saint David's Day, aren't you, love? Isn't that in March?" asks a man after Gran waves a daffodil vigorously in his face.

"As a matter of fact, I'm selling these daffodils to

raise money for the Marie Curie hospice around the corner," Gran tells him, giving him a Medusa-like look that could turn a mere mortal to stone. "My daughter Laura, Kitty's mother, died there earlier this year. I'm not standing on Hampstead High Street to celebrate the patron saint of Wales. I've never even been to Wales, and yes, Saint David's Day is in March."

She stops talking and waits while the man, who looked more and more uncomfortable with every word, reaches into his wallet and produces a twenty-pound note, which he stuffs into the collection box.

"Many thanks," Gran says cheerfully as he disappears up the hill at a rapid pace.

"Gran! You made that poor man feel awful."

"Well, he gave us twenty pounds. If guilt encourages people to be more generous, then I'm not above taking advantage of that for a good cause. Saint David's Day indeed, what an idiotic comment!"

Her next victims are an unsuspecting Italian family. They raise their hands apologetically explaining they only have Euros.

"I accept all currencies," says Gran and stands there until the father drops a ten-euro note into her tin. She really is shameless, which she says is the main reason she's the hospice's top fundraiser.

"I think I'll get one of those mobile card swipers," she says after the fifth person tells us they don't have any cash on them. "Fewer and fewer people seem to carry cash these days. Remind me to have a look online when we get back to the house."

We walk down the hill toward home. Sir Lancelot, who is panting alongside us, doesn't seem to be missing his owner too much. In fact, he looks almost cheerful in the fading light. Perhaps he's relieved to be out of the kitchen, or maybe he knows it's suppertime.

"It seems like just yesterday that Laura was your age," says Gran, smiling down at me. "You remind me of her so much. Imogen looks more like her, but your personality is so similar to your mum's. You have her sense of humor and her sense of fairness. You're a wonderful listener, just like your mother. I'll never stop missing Laura, but at least I get to see glimpses of her every day in you and your sister."

I squeeze Gran's hand, not sure how to respond. That's why people think I'm a good listener, not because I am but because I often don't know what to say.

"Someone at the hospice told me that grief is like glitter," Gran says. "If you throw a handful of glitter in the air, even if you try your very best to clean it up, you'll never get it all. I think that's true. I keep finding glitter tucked into unexpected corners. I suppose it will always be there."

I lie in bed that night pondering Gran's grief glitter. It's true. There are little piles of it waiting to be found everywhere.

Mrs. Allison arrives back from filming the first episode, bursting to tell us about her weekend. She's signed something called a nondisclosure agreement, so she's supposed to keep most of what happened a secret. Gran snorts when she hears that.

"It's hardly the MI5, is it? Her Majesty's secret baking service!"

Mrs. Allison ignores Gran and tells us that her Saint Clement's orange and lemon drizzle cake was a big hit, the technical challenge, where you don't get to know what you'll be baking beforehand, was a bit of a nightmare, but her signature bake of a trio of chocolate sponges was a triumph.

"That's probably more detail than I should have told you," she says, looking nervously around the kitchen as if a team of lawyers might leap out from a cupboard.

We sit down together the following week to watch the first episode. Mrs. Allison's Zumba friends are having a viewing party, complete with cakes, streamers, and life-size cutouts of the judges, but it turns out that the Zumba teacher has a dog phobia, so Sir Lancelot couldn't have attended.

"Imagine someone being scared of my little boo-boo," she says, scratching his forehead.

"It is hard to imagine," says Gran, examining Sir Lancelot's flat little face. "He hardly looks as if he's going to spring at someone, does he?"

"Anyway," Mrs. Allison continues, ignoring Gran, "the Zumba crew is together at Maude's place, and I'm here with all of you and Sir Lancelot, which is much nicer."

We settle down around the television with a pot of tea and a range of baked goods. It's Pie Week filming next weekend, so the coffee table is laden with Mrs. Allison's planned signature bake of two pies, one sweet and one savory. Imogen and I both refuse to taste the savory pie because it has gross things in it like rabbit, pheasant, and venison.

"I wonder if dog pie is a thing," I say.

"Kitty, don't say that in front of Sir Lancelot!" Mrs. Allison squeals, putting her arms around him to protect him from potential dog bakers.

"You could make a few pies out of him," says Dad, placing another forkful of venison pie in his mouth. Mrs. Allison glares at him.

"Sorry," he mutters through the crumbs.

Deeply regretting my dog comment, I pat Mrs. Allison on the shoulder.

"I think this apple and plum pie is one of your best," I tell her, which must placate her because she cuts me another large slice.

"Of course, the biggest challenge in Pie Week is Paul's constant checking for a soggy bottom. Having a soggy bottom could get you sent home like that!" Mrs. Allison snaps her fingers dramatically in Dad's face, and he spills his tea.

"A soggy what?" he asks, mopping his tea-soaked trousers with a napkin.

"A soggy bottom. The base of the pie has to be dry and crisp. There can't be any leakage. Don't you remember that poor woman last year whose filling came out?"

Dad looks alarmed and peeks under his slice of game pie.

"Dry as a bone," he says.

I check underneath my pie. It is a bit soggy. Well, maybe damp rather than soggy. I decide not to mention it, since I don't want to upset Mrs. Allison again after my dog pie comment.

The contestants are introduced one by one, and suddenly Mrs. Allison appears on the screen, larger than life and resplendent in her lime-green M&S blouse and a pristine white apron. She's whisking her cake mixture vigorously while talking to the two judges.

"This is one of my favorite cakes to bake," she says, "and the little girls who live next door to me absolutely love it."

We whoop in delight at getting a mention, even though she did describe us as little girls.

"Well, they're not the judges today, so let's see what we think of it, shall we Lizzie?" asks Paul ominously as he moves on to the next contestant. "Good luck."

"Do we like that man?" asks Gran, eyeing him suspiciously. "Obviously we're fond of Prue, but I'm not sure about him. What kind of last name is Hollywood anyway? Presumably it's a stage name. What are his credentials?"

"It's his real name," says Mrs. Allison, "I asked him. He was head baker at some fancy London hotel, and bread is his specialty. The crew makes lots of jokes about him looking like a silverback gorilla, which he has quite a good sense of humor about, considering."

"A bit too close to home, I would think," says Gran. "You know, this is really rather a good show. I think I'll keep on watching even after you get eliminated."

Imogen pokes Gran to indicate this wasn't the most tactful comment, and we all go back to watching television and munching pie. Sir Lancelot has managed to snaffle some game pie and has hidden under the table with it. He apparently doesn't mind eating Bambi. The episode concludes with a retired Welsh accountant named Rhys being sent home for his runny chocolate soufflé.

"Nice chap," says Mrs. Allison, "awful to be the first one sent home. He was terribly upset."

"He looked relieved to me," Dad says. "It seems like hard work, this baking business. Now he can relax at home watching you lot sweating your socks off in that tent, while he has a cold beer and a store-bought pork pie sitting on his sofa. He's not going to need to worry about having a soggy bottom!"

Well, Rhys may be able to relax now, but I can't. Not until Mrs. Allison is crowned the greatest British baker. I can't wait to see the trophy.

CHAPTER NINE

BAKING BITES BACK

Mrs. Allison continues to triumph in episode after episode of *The Great British Bake Off*, but when things go wrong five weeks later, they go badly wrong. We gather in the living room to watch the semifinals. Although Mrs. Allison isn't allowed to tell us what happened at filming, her gloomy face and red eyes when she arrived home late last Sunday evening said it all. For once, there are no cakes or pies on the coffee table. Our next-door neighbor hasn't baked all week and sits next to me looking glum and nursing a glass of brandy. Still, here we all are, staring at the television, hoping for a different outcome than the one we suspect. My fingers are crossed underneath the stretched-out sleeves of my sweatshirt, which Gran keeps telling me to pull up. Even Cleo joins us, sitting on the bookshelf so that she can keep a disdainful eye on Sir Lancelot.

Today we have a new member of the viewing party, Josh, Imogen's boyfriend. He's always here these days, hanging out in the kitchen or living room, gangly legs flung over chair arms, and ridiculously large shoes kicked off in the hallway. Josh's blond hair flops annoyingly over his left eye, and he's constantly restyling it. He wears jeans that hang down, revealing white boxer shorts. Mrs. Allison says that at least they look clean. Josh doesn't work well as Ponytail Girl's love interest, who, in my mind, should have brooding, midnight eyes, and jet-black hair, in contrast to her golden beauty. He could be called Raven Boy. Nobody would ever invent a superhero called Floppy Hair Boy. Imogen thinks Josh is fantastic, though. Gran and Dad have had several heated discussions about the suitability of Imogen having a boyfriend at her age, which I listened in on.

"She is thirteen, Eleanor, and he seems like a nice enough boy. They meet at Starbucks after school to hang out."

"Well, we didn't let Laura have a boyfriend until she was sixteen," says Gran.

"You may not have let her, but I distinctly remember her telling me that she had her first kiss when she was fourteen with the brother of her French pen pal. What was his name? François? Sébastien? Anyway, it put her off French men for life, which was lucky for me."

"I told her father she was too young for that trip. The French girl who came to stay with us chain-smoked Marlboro Lights, with her parents' permission. Imagine that! Of course, we made her smoke out in the garden, which she complained about to her mum and dad on the phone. I don't think she realized I speak fluent French, considering some of the language she used to describe me."

On the television, Mrs. Allison lights up the screen in her aqua and lilac blouse, her dazzling TV smile in stark contrast to her gloomy face next to me.

"I should never have worn that shirt," she says. "I was going to save it for the final. I jinxed myself."

We watch as Mrs. Allison sails through the first two challenges of the semifinal. It's hard to imagine what could possibly go wrong, but as the showstopper round starts, things begin to unravel, and the mood darkens. It's awful to watch someone you care about struggling, and in front of the whole country, which makes it even worse. The television seems to be growing, and as Mrs. Allison's face gets bigger and bigger on the screen, she seems to be getting smaller and smaller on the sofa. On TV, an ugly flush of redness creeps up her chest and neck, clashing with her lilac and aqua shirt as she begins to lose the battle with the cake. Sir Lancelot whines, turns his back on the baking show, and rests his triple chin on his owner's lap.

"I can't watch," she says, hiding behind a cushion. "That gateau Saint Honoré was a triumph when I made it for you, Kitty, wasn't it? A triumph." She sounds as if she's going to cry.

"It was perfect," I say, uncrossing my fingers and giving her hand a little squeeze.

"And Saint Honoré is the patron saint of baking," she wails.

"Have another drink, Elizabeth," says Gran, pouring all the grown-ups a generous slug of brandy.

The judging begins, and when it's Mrs. Allison's turn to carry her cake up to the judging table, we all hold our breath.

"Well, Lizzie," says Paul. "What happened here?"

"I don't know," she says. "The puff pastry wasn't right, and everything went downhill from there. I'm sorry. It's the worst thing I've ever made!" Mrs. Allison is clearly on the verge of tears.

Sir Lancelot turns his head and growls at Paul Hollywood, before settling his chins back down on Mrs. Allison's knee. I know how he feels.

"Don't upset yourself, dear," says Prue. "It does look lovely, although, as you say, the pastry is all wrong. I must say we have come to expect more from you, Elizabeth. This is quite a disappointment."

"I've always found someone saying something is a disappointment to be unspeakably patronizing," says Gran, refilling Mrs. Allison's glass. "Girls, doesn't she remind you of your headmistress?"

"Oh my God, yes!" says Imogen. "That is so Mrs. Brooks. 'Imogen, dear, not only have you let yourself down by wearing lip gloss, you have let down the whole community here at Haverstock Girls' School. I'm not angry, I'm disappointed.'"

"Shhhh," I hiss. "I'm trying to watch."

As the judges deliberate, it becomes clear that Mrs. Allison is at risk. The only other contestant who had a bad round is a smug gray-haired man called Graham, who is sporting a red and white polka-dot bow tie. According to the judges, his puff pastry was flakier.

"However impressive Lizzie's baking has been this season, we can't put someone through to the final who hasn't mastered a full puff pastry," says Paul into the camera.

Mrs. Allison tries and fails to hide a sob.

"I made choux pastry *and* puff. None of the other contestants had two types of pastry."

"Let's switch it off," says Gran, briskly picking up the

remote control. "I don't care who wins if Elizabeth isn't part of the show."

"Graham wins," Mrs. Allison says sadly.

"Well, there you go then, I never did meet a Graham I liked," says Gran and clinks her glass with Mrs. Allison's.

And so ends Mrs. Allison's baking dream and the fifty or so minutes each week when we sat down together and almost felt like a real family again. Now, what are we going to do?

CHAPTER TEN

THE BIG APPLE

"Girls, I have something I want to discuss with you," Dad calls up the stairs. In my experience when a parent has something they would like to discuss with you, it almost certainly means they are about to tell you something that a) you are not going to like, and b) they have already decided, so instead of saying "something to discuss with you," they should say "something to tell you."

"What's up?" says Imogen. "I'm in the middle of getting ready to see Josh."

I study my sister's face, and she is not kidding when she says she's halfway through her beauty routine. She has one perfectly smoky eye carefully shaded from Elephant's Breath—color 229—to Dove Tale—number 267—and ending in Down Pipe—color number 26. The result is an exquisite black eye, which looks as if she has been hit in the face by a volleyball, and the bruising created this stunning result that a Hollywood actress would pay a fortune for. The other eye is unadorned. I like her makeup-free eye the best. Imogen is one of those people who wakes up looking like the *Teen Vogue* model for the "barely there" makeup feature. When I wake up with my hair sticking out on one side, my cheek creased with an angry line of red from the edge of my pillow and half-closed puffy eyes, I look like the "barely cares" feature.

I drag my gaze away from Imogen's mismatched eyes and study Dad. He is rocking from foot to foot, managing to look excited and nervous at the same time. I have a feeling that what he is about to say is not going to be good—not good at all.

"I have great news," he says.

I'll be the judge of that.

"A wonderful opportunity has come up for us to spend a few months living in New York City! Can you believe it?"

No, actually, I cannot believe it. I stand gawping at Dad until Imogen's squeal of excitement breaks the stunned silence.

"Are you serious?" she asks him, hopping up and down excitedly. What with Dad's rocking and her hopping, they look like they're warming up for a race.

"One hundred percent serious. My company needs someone to run a project in the New York office, and I'm the lucky one. We're the lucky ones!"

"This is so awesome. I can't wait to tell Lily," Imogen says. "Bright lights, big city, and the shopping!"

I have a thousand things running through my head, and none of them includes a wardrobe upgrade, which is obviously at the top of Imogen's list.

"What about school? What about Gran? We can't leave her. Who will look after Cleo? What about Jess? I won't have any friends. I don't know anyone there. I don't want to go. I'm not going." As I speak, I can feel my face getting redder, and my voice starting to wobble. The all-too-familiar spring of tears prickles behind my eyes, but these aren't sad tears; these are angry tears. How could Dad seriously consider taking me away from everything I have left in the world? I turn and run up the stairs, slamming the door to my bedroom so hard that half a dozen books fall off the shelf.

Dad follows me and tries to explain that it's only for a few months, that he's already talked to Mrs. Brooks, and Imogen and I will go back to Haverstock Girls' School in January, that Gran is happy for us and thinks the change will do us a world of good and that she will look after Cleo, and that Jess and everyone else will still be here when we get back. After forty-five minutes of being patient, he loses his temper when I tell him for the forty-sixth time that I will not be going to New York.

"Kitty, you are coming. End of discussion," he says and shuts the door. He doesn't slam it, but I can tell that he wanted to.

The following day Lily comes over, and I eavesdrop as Imogen tells her all about Josh's reaction to her leaving London.

"He wasn't exactly crying when I told him about New York, but I could tell he wanted to because his eyes looked all shiny," she says, sniffing.

"Oh my God, that's so romantic," says Lily.

I'm not sure how or why that would be considered romantic. It sounds pretty pathetic to me. What's Josh got to cry about? He's not the one having to uproot his whole life and move to New York. Apparently, my sister and Floppy Hair Boy are going to make things work in what Imogen irritatingly describes as a "transatlantic relationship."

"I mean, it's going to be hard, but we're both really committed to making a long-distance relationship work," Imogen says.

I roll my eyes and decide to call Kate. At least she'll be on my side.

"Kitty, your mum would be thrilled for you!" she

practically screams down the phone. "Laura and I went on holiday to New York together years ago. She loved it so much I thought I was never going to persuade her to come home. I've got some photos in the attic at Honeystone House. I'll have to dig them out for you. Are you excited?"

Nope.

I call Jess, whose reaction is almost as annoying as Kate's, but in a very different way.

"How can your dad do this to me? You're my best friend! You should come and live with me. Mum and Dad won't mind, and you can help me look after the fox family. I can't believe you're leaving me on my own."

"This isn't about you, Jess! You're not the one who has to move to another country where you don't know anyone. I'll have to go to a new school. Probably one with boys."

"With boys? Really?"

Jessica sounds wistful at the idea of going to a school with boys. She is quite keen on having a boyfriend and says the only boys she knows are her little brother's friends, who are all eight years old. She quickly gets back to the matter in hand.

"Well, who am I supposed to sit next to at school if you live in America? I don't like anyone else in our class. I'm starting an online petition, or a GoFundMe page, or both. I was going to do one to raise money for a fox sanctuary, but I'll do one to keep you in London."

"What would we use the money for?"

"I don't know. A lawyer or something? This is a clear violation of your human rights, Kitty. You can emancipate yourself."

"I don't want to emancipate myself. I just don't want to move to New York. It's not fair."

"Then what are you going to do about it?" she asks.

"I'm going to make a list of all the reasons this is a terrible idea and present it to Dad."

Dad always says I react to things without thinking them through, so this time I'll make a well-reasoned and calm presentation of the indisputable fact that this is the worst idea he has ever had. Ever.

I spend the next few days producing a set of slides to ensure the whole thing looks professional. My arguments are wide-ranging and well researched, and when Jess and I review the presentation, we're both confident that it makes a compelling case. The best slide is the one where I list some of the most unpleasant things about life in New York City.

1. There are rats so big that they can pull slices of pizza up subway stairs. See image below.

2. I read an interview with a woman who saw a man poo on the subway. Fortunately, there is no image for this.

3. They have hurricanes, deadly floods, fatal heat waves, snowstorms, and even earthquakes in New York. Scientists predict a magnitude five earthquake is imminent, which would generate more than thirty million tons of rubble! You do not want to be in the subway when that happens, even if nobody is going to the loo. I include a picture of the devastating effects of an earthquake. Admittedly this photo was taken in Japan, but I think it makes the point nicely.

4. A pigeon once got into a subway car and went crazy. See link to video. Dad is super scared of pigeons, or flying rats, as he calls them, and once had a panic attack in Trafalgar Square when one landed on his head. Dominic was with us and laughed so much he said he peed his pants. Dad is going to freak out.

5. There are twice as many murders in New

York City per annum than in London. It
is hard to imagine a parent who would
move their family there out of choice.

Although this statistic speaks for itself, I feel the need
to add the second sentence.

"Wow!" says Jess. "Well done, Kitty. The presentation
is absolutely amazing and terrifying. Your dad will flip
out. He hates pigeons, doesn't he?"

That weekend I call an emergency family meeting with
just one agenda item: "New York, New York: No Way, No
How." When I open Dad's laptop, which I've borrowed
for the occasion, Imogen rolls her eyes, but Dad smiles
encouragingly. His smile fades and his face pales when
he sees the video of the pigeon flapping wildly around
the subway car, so I play it three times. I do find it trou-
bling that this is the thing that seems to concern him the
most. Imogen, unmoved by Pizza Rat or the impending
earthquake, pushes her chair back and waves her hand
dismissively, as if my presentation and I are annoying
insects.

"Thank you for the presentation, Kitty," Dad says
when some of the color has returned to his cheeks. "I
appreciate you taking the time to share your thoughts,

but this isn't going to change my mind. We will be moving to New York at the end of August."

"Yes!" says Imogen, giving me a triumphant look.

"We don't even have a place to live," I say, desperate to find a reason to stop or at least delay the move.

"Yes, we do," Dad says, grinning. "I've found us a fantastic apartment. Pass the laptop. I can show you some photos. It's on the twenty-fourth floor, and it's got the most amazing view."

"Does the building have a doorman?" Imogen asks.

A doorman? Clearly, the poor girl has her priorities all wrong. Didn't she pay attention to the presentation? Magnitude five earthquake plus twenty-fourth-floor apartment equals certain death. For a so-called straight-A student, she can be a bit slow at times.

"There's an entire team of doormen," Dad says. "Twenty-four hours a day, seven days a week. I can imagine it now, Imogen." Dad does a bad imitation of an American accent. "Good morning, Miss Wentworth, have a nice day."

"Everyone knows Americans are fake friendly. English people might be grumpy, but they do care, deep down," I say. I can feel my face getting hot and angry tears rushing to my eyes. "So that's it then? We're going?"

"Why do you have to be so miserable about everything,

Kitty?" Imogen says, slapping her palm on the table. "This is the first good thing that's happened to us in ages, and just because you don't like the idea of moving, you have to ruin it for everyone else."

"Imo, don't be angry with Kitty. It is a big move, and I understand that she's nervous. It will be a huge change for all of us, but I really think it will be a good thing for our family, Kitty. Your mum loved it there." He looks around the kitchen sadly. "We need a change of scenery. We need to have something to look forward to. I need that, and I think when you get over your nerves, you'll see that I'm right."

"I hate you!" I push my chair back, and the metal legs squeak painfully across the wooden floor. Dad winces, whether at the noise or at my words, I don't know. I've never said that to Dad before. As I lie in bed that night unable to sleep, thoughts of unfamiliar streets, faces, and voices tumbling around my head, I try not to think about the look on Dad's face.

The following evening I log into Flying Solo. I haven't been there for a while, but I notice the same old names. Sure enough, Dad has been very active over the past month. I go straight to his saved posts and read the most recent one.

"Hi! I'm hoping there are a few New Yorkers out there who can give me some advice. I'm planning a move from London to NYC with my daughters, and am looking for recs for a family-friendly neighborhood with good schools. Any tips would be much appreciated. It's exciting but all a bit overwhelming. TIA! WWLD."

There is a flurry of responses:

"I've never been but lucky you!"

"Hi WWLD! New Yorker here. Property prices in NYC are insane. Check out New Jersey."

"I'd love to live in London. We should do a house swap!"

"Three words: Upper West Side. Good schools and close to the park."

"Good luck, WWLD! Keep us posted!"

I decide to post a reply from my own account.

"This sounds like a terrible idea. Are you seriously planning on taking your daughters away from everything they know? Everything that makes them feel safe? Wow, just wow! If you have to move to New York, perhaps your daughters could stay with a relative or friend? Sorry to say this but you sound selfish. Good luck, MMM."

When I check back later, my post has seventeen dislikes and only one like, which I gave to myself. I bet the people on Flying Solo wouldn't want to be dragged to the other side of the world. Why does everything keep changing? Why can't everything be like it was before? Why is nobody on my side?

CHAPTER ELEVEN

DAYROOM YELLOW

I try to process the fact that in just a few weeks, I will no longer be living in London but in New York City. Sam and I have spent hours discussing the move, and at today's appointment, it's evident that I am all talked out. There are only so many times I can rant about pigeons, earthquakes, Imogen, and Dad.

"Kitty, sometimes in order to move forward, we need to look back," Sam says. He obviously feels that we've exhausted the New York topic of conversation. Maybe he's just bored of me. I wouldn't blame him. I'm boring myself. I often do lately.

"So, today, I'd like us to talk about those last few weeks with your mum. Do you remember how you felt when she moved into the hospice?"

The hospice is a place I have tried and failed miserably to erase from my memory. It's just a few streets away from our house, and I've been walking the long way to my appointments with Sam to avoid it ever since Mum died. Apparently, it's one of the best hospices in London. Perhaps the real estate agents of Belsize Park should include that in the selling points for local properties: "this delightful home is situated in a peaceful, leafy corner of North London, and conveniently located for the Tube station, the shops, and a lovely hospice, perfect for when your time comes."

The hospice is in a bright, modern building full of potted plants and with cheery paintings of vases of flowers hanging on the yellow walls. If they'd used Farrow & Ball paint to decorate, it would have been Dayroom Yellow, color 233, but I suspect they used a cheaper brand. It is a surprisingly cheerful and lively place, given it's somewhere you go to die. There's even a tiny hairdressing salon. Volunteers come in to paint patients' nails, read, or just sit by the bed of people who don't have any visitors. I always thought that was weird. Imagine waking up with a complete stranger sitting next to your bed, reading to you. What if you didn't like the book they'd chosen?

Mum had her own room, and there was a shared family room across the hallway with a small kitchen, a couple of sofas, a television, and, bizarrely, an electronic piano that I never heard anyone play. I always wondered about that piano and how and why it ended up there. Sam had visited Mum at the hospice, so he knows all about the yellow walls, the hairdressing salon, and the piano. What he wants me to talk about is what those last weeks of Mum's life were like for me.

I shiver at the memory of my first visit to the hospice. Mum looked so pale and thin and was trying hard not to cough. She invited me to climb up onto her bed while Gran fussed around her. Gran was always there, bustling around the room moving flowers, tissues, pillows, and books. The last few days, though, she suddenly became still and sat in the chair next to Mum's bed staring at her, only moving to let another visitor take the seat before resuming her silent vigil.

"Does Gran sleep here?" I asked Dad once.

"Sometimes. The nurses try to persuade her to go home to get a decent night's sleep in her own bed, but she tells them she can't sleep at her house, so they let her stay."

"Can I sleep here?" I didn't think I wanted to but wanted to know what Dad would say.

"No, love. Mum specifically asked me to make sure that we all sleep at home. She says it makes her happy to think of you, Imogen, and me tucked up in our beds."

★ ★ ★

"Kitty!" says Sam, bringing me back from the family room at the hospice to his office. Funny, I never noticed the similarities in the wall color.

"Is this paint Dayroom Yellow?"

"I have no idea. Let's not discuss the decor. We were talking about the time at the hospice before Laura died."

Sam always says *death*, *cancer*, *terminal*, and other words that most people try to avoid using in front of me. He says it's important to give things their proper names. I suppose not using scary words is as pointless as trying to avoid saying Voldemort's name. It doesn't protect you from anything.

"If I tell you I don't remember lots of things, you should believe me, because it's true. Some things are so vivid, though, like the smell of the flowers in the room and how Mum looked smaller each visit, as if the bed around her was growing. I remember that we ran out of tissues a lot in the family room and that when I went to the nurses' station to get more, they said what a good thing it was to let it all out. I remember walking into Mum's room once and seeing her sitting up in bed with Dad holding her. I thought maybe she was feeling better since she hadn't sat up in days, but she wasn't. I remember when Dad told us that the doctors said she would probably soon be gone. I remember wondering every time I kissed her goodbye if it would be the last time. I remember the last time, even though I didn't know it was the last time then, if you see what I mean."

"I do see, Kitty. You remember a lot and did really well talking about it," Sam says. "How do you feel?"

"Awful."

"Therapy can be a bit like Snakes and Ladders."

"What do you mean?"

"It has its ups and downs. Ironically, what feels like a snake is often a ladder when processing grief. By the way—do you know that the game Snakes and Ladders is called Chutes and Ladders in the States? You need to know these things since you'll be living there for a few months," Sam says.

"No, I didn't, and I still don't know what you're talking about. How is grief like Snakes and Ladders, or 'Chutes' and Ladders?" I put the word *chutes* into air quotes and roll my eyes.

"Well, sometimes the biggest fall equals the most progress. Do you know what I mean?"

"No. Can I go now, please?"

Sam smiles. "Of course. Your dad's waiting outside. Well done, Kitty. You're doing brilliantly. I'm proud of you, and I know that your mum would be too."

✶ ✶ ✶

As Dad and I walk the familiar route home, I try to count how many appointments I've had with Sam in the four months since Mum died. Usually one a week, sometimes two, let's say six times a month, so twenty-four appointments. I have no idea whether Sam told Dad he was planning on talking to me about Mum's time at the hospice today or not. Is Sam even allowed to talk about what I say in my appointments? I have a hazy memory of him telling me in one of our first sessions that our conversations would be private unless my well-being were at stake. I never asked him what he meant by that. I trust Sam to do the right thing. I don't want to keep secrets that could harm me.

Usually, I ignore the turn to the right, the one that leads to the hospice. Ever since Mum died, I've held my breath while I crossed that road, studiously avoiding it, only breathing again when it was behind me. Today though, I take Dad's hand and turn right. He looks down at me, but I don't meet his gaze, instead staring straight ahead as the redbrick building appears in front of us. We stop wordlessly at the entrance to the driveway, which is flanked on either side by tall glossy green privet hedges. There are a few cars parked next to the building, but there isn't a soul to be seen. I stare up at the window of the corner room on the third floor, which was Mum's room. Dad follows my gaze and pulls me into him. He's so much thinner than he was. I didn't notice it until I saw some photos of him before Mum got ill. Mum was so tiny in those last few months that he seemed like a comforting giant next to her. In reality, he got smaller too. Perhaps he does need this move. Perhaps we all do. Perhaps it will be a relief not to expect to see Mum around every corner.

"I'm sorry, Dad," I whisper. "For what I said. I could never hate you."

"I know that, my love. It's going to be okay. You never know, you might even enjoy New York."

"Just until the end of the year?"

"Just until the end of the year."

Dad takes my hand, and we continue home. For the first time in a very long time, I've taken the most direct route and walked right past the pain.

CHAPTER TWELVE

CAKE FOR BREAKFAST

We are spending my birthday weekend at my godmother's house in the Cotswolds. I love Honeystone House. During the week, Kate lives in an apartment near Marylebone High Street, in London, but Kate, her husband, Matt, and her moody Russian blue cat, Pasha, spend most weekends at Honeystone House, which is as beautiful on the inside as it is out. Kate is an interior designer, and Honeystone was in *Elle Decor* and *Homes & Gardens* magazines. There was a glossy spread of pictures of the outside of the house, along with photos of Kate wafting around her living room wearing a gauzy white kaftan, acting as if she's cooking in the kitchen, and looking pensive and expensive sitting on the window seat in the master bedroom pretending to read. We always laugh at that picture, since Kate noticed after it was taken that the book was upside down.

I always sleep in the Peony room when we stay here. All the bedrooms in Kate's house are named after flowers and painted the color of their petals. Matt refuses to call the rooms by their names. He says it's pretentious. Instead, he calls them "the second biggest bedroom" or "the one where the radiator needs checking." Dad sleeps in the Primrose room, and Imogen sleeps in the Bluebell room, which she loves because of the enormous clawfoot bathtub. She spends hours in there using up whole bottles of expensive bubble bath. Kate says she doesn't mind, but I would if I were her.

Each bedroom is painted in the Farrow & Ball shade closest to the flower it's named after. In the Bluebell room, this is number 220, Pitch Blue. The Primrose room is painted in Pale Hound, number 71, and Peony is decorated in Nancy's Blushes. Nancy's Blushes, color number 278, is described on the website as "a true pink named after the scrumptious rosy cheeks of a much-loved little girl called Nancy." It's funny to think that Nancy is probably an old lady now. I hope her cheeks are still scrumptious. Farrow & Ball has the absolute best paint names.

Kate and my mum are equally responsible for my obsession with Farrow & Ball's paint colors and names. When I was little, Kate would give me thrillingly sharp pairs of scissors, which I used to painstakingly cut out the small colored squares from stacks of paint charts. I would sit next to her, surrounded by colors, wallpaper samples, and swatches of linen, silk, and velvet while she worked on mood boards for her clients. There's a photo of the two of us that Mum took, both with our heads down, concentrating hard. In the picture, Kate is prettily biting her lip, and I have my tongue stuck in my right cheek, a sure sign of hard work. I would point to a color, and Mum would tell me the name from the chart. Mum liked to read aloud the color's origin story from the website. She said it made paint much more interesting when there is a backstory to make you daydream about Edwardian drawing rooms, the moors of Scotland or, in the case of India Yellow, "the pigment collected from the urine of cows fed on a special diet of mango leaves." That is one of the best color descriptions ever.

Kate helped me decorate my bedroom using paint from dozens of tiny tester jars, as I couldn't pick a favorite. As well as the loveliest colors, I chose the ones with the most magical names, like Skimming Stone, Babouche, which is named after the color of Moroccan slippers, Elephant's Breath, Charlotte's Locks, and Arsenic. Arsenic! What an absolutely brilliant name for a shade of paint. It was named after the bright green of the wallpaper in Napoleon's bathroom, which contained arsenic and slowly poisoned him. I want to work as a creator of paint when I'm older. Kate said I would make a "discerning colorist," so that is what I call my chosen profession. People always look at me strangely when I tell them that's what I want to be when I grow up, as if it's not even a real job. Well, it is, and I've already started on my portfolio of colors. Some of my ideas are Unicorn's Tears, which is a soft white with a tiny hint of silver, Whimsy, the palest aqua, Owl Feather, a yellowish-brown, and Kate's Contrary Kitten which is the color of the fur underneath Pasha's chin. Kate says they are all amazing, and she helped me write a letter to Farrow & Ball with these suggestions along with blended watercolors to show the approximate shades. We sent it ages ago, and I haven't had a reply yet, which has really annoyed Kate. She says she's going to switch to a different designer paint brand if I don't hear back this month. I won't let her.

I wake up early on my eleventh birthday. I'm happy to be eleven, because ten was the worst year ever. Last night Pasha gifted me the great honor of sleeping on my bed, but as soon as I sit up, he gives me a baleful, green-eyed glare, springs off the mattress, and pads downstairs. I follow him through the silent house and find Dad sitting in the kitchen, drinking an enormous mug of tea.

"Happy birthday, Kitty-Cat. It's still very early. How

did you sleep?" Dad pulls me in close for a hug, and his stubble catches on my hair.

"Why are you up so early?" I ask.

"Well, this time eleven years ago I had a completely sleepless night, and I've woken up early on your birthday ever since. It was six a.m. when you finally graced us with your presence."

"Tell me again about when I was born." I've heard this story a hundred times but love it, and Dad never seems to get tired of telling it.

"Well, Mum was determined to have a natural birth, even though I pointed out that she wouldn't choose to get her wisdom teeth removed without an anesthetic, and after your sister was born, she vowed she would take every drug on offer. Of course, she decided we should walk to the hospital. When we got to the bottom of the hill, it was obvious that she wasn't going to make it to the top.

"'I'll run home and get the car,' I said. 'You wait here.'

"'No! Rob, you can't leave me. Look, there's a cab at the traffic light.'

"Sure enough, the friendly glow of the orange sign showed the taxi was available, although I seriously doubted the cabbie would stop to pick up a woman who was clearly on the verge of giving birth, and a hysterical-looking man. I jumped into the street in front of the cab, offered him twenty pounds to drive us to the top of the hill, and, miracle of miracles, he agreed.

"'Bloody hell, love!' the driver said, turning around to get a good look at Mum. 'Can you hold it in for ten minutes so we can get you to the hospital and into a nice bed?' In a lower voice, he whispered to me, 'My wife's had four babies, and I'm telling you, mate, she's about to pop.'

"'I can hear you,' Laura shouted. 'I'm pregnant, not deaf. Now shut up and bloody drive!'

"When we screeched up to the hospital entrance, I leaped out of the cab and raced inside to get a doctor, nurse, porter, basically anyone I could find who was wearing a uniform. When I got back to the taxi a few minutes later with a nurse and a porter pushing a wheelchair, Laura was standing by the cab calmly chatting with the driver. This made my frantic screaming of 'The baby's coming, the baby's coming!' seem overly dramatic, and the nurse rolled her eyes at the porter as she helped Mum into the wheelchair.

"'Good luck, darling!' shouted the cab driver. 'Get them to give you plenty of gas and air. My name's Frank, by the way, if it's a boy.'

"And thirty minutes later, you arrived." Dad grins at me and ruffles my hair.

I smile as I always do when I hear the story of Frank

and the mad dash to the hospital. Every time we take a taxi, I ask the driver his name, just in case it's Frank— then I'll be able to tell him that I am Kitty Frances Wentworth, who was almost born in the back of his spotless cab.

We wait until everyone else is awake before I open my presents. Kate bustles around the kitchen with Matt, producing bowls of freshly picked raspberries and blueberries from the garden, croissants warmed in the oven, and cups of hot chocolate with tiny marshmallows bobbing in the foam. Kate places the birthday cake Mrs. Allison made for me in the center of the table, and we all admire its splendor. The cake is in the shape of an artist's palette, made from vanilla sponge with seven cookie paint jars each filled with different colored custard. There are three intricate chocolate paintbrushes, which you can dip into the custards to taste the different flavors: vanilla, cherry, mango, lemon and lime, peanut butter, chocolate, and toffee. I love it!

"Mrs. Allison would have had a winner with this cake on that baking show," says Matt.

"If the god of baking hadn't turned on her," says Dad. "That made for the most awkward television viewing ever!"

Kate gives him a friendly smack on the shoulder and

tells him to be quiet and light the candles.

Birthday breakfast has included cake for as long as I can remember. Mum said it was a way to make sure that the whole family got to sing, blow out candles, and eat cake together on the big day.

"Evenings were always so busy with work, school, ballet, swimming lessons, baths, and bedtime. When you were small you and Imogen used to go to bed at eight, Dad didn't get home from work until after six, and there was no way I was going to give you a sugar rush just before bedtime. Hyperactive toddlers can be entertaining in the morning but not so much at ten at night, so cake for breakfast became our thing."

On top of the pretty heap of presents and cards is the cream envelope with "Kitty's 11th Birthday" written on it in Mum's purple swirly handwriting. I pass it to Dad.

"Can you keep it for me for later? I'm not ready yet," I say.

Dad sets the letter softly on the shelf behind him.

"It's there for you whenever you want to read it, my love."

As soon as everyone has wandered off to various parts of the house, I slip back into the kitchen and grab the letter. I want to be on my own when I read it, so I head out of the back door and go to my favorite part of the garden, the enormous weeping willow tree. It's as tall as a house, and I always feel safe in its leafy embrace. With the letter on my lap, I sit there for a while, listening to the sounds of the garden and watching the chinks of sunlight peep between the leaves. My hands are trembling when I pick up the envelope, and I open it as carefully as I can, trying not to tear it as I remove the folded paper and open the letter. A small package tumbles into my lap. It is wrapped neatly in tissue paper, which is exactly the same color as a newborn chick. I decide to read the letter first. Gran always taught us that it is impolite to open the present before the card, so I always open the card first and study it for five seconds, a respectful amount of time, before unwrapping the present. In the familiar, loopy handwriting that I've seen hundreds of times before on shopping lists pinned to the kitchen bulletin board, or Post-its stuck on the table saying things like "buy butter," "dentist at 4," or "Cleo to vet," Mum wrote:

My darling Kitty,

I've started this letter about twenty times already, but Dad says I have to get on with it, so this will be the one. Also, I'm feeling guilty about wasting all this lovely writing paper, so here we go.

First of all, happy, happy eleventh birthday, my gorgeous girl! I love you so much and wish you a year full of sunshine, smiles, and adventures.

When I first talked to Dad about writing these letters for you and Imogen to open on your birthdays, I told him the three rules I am determined to stick to:

1. I'll keep the letters brief—two pages ideally. As my English teacher used to say, "brevity is next to godliness."

2. I'll do my very best not to make them maudlin. (If you don't know what that word means, please look it up later ☺.) My goal is to make you smile, not shed a tear. Crying is fine though, in fact, the therapist in me would say that doing both is the healthiest response. The mum in me just wants the smiles.

3. Every year I'll give you a charm for your bracelet and write a little bit about what it means, which will hopefully keep me on track for rules one and two.

You should open the present now. I bet you waited!

Inside the tissue paper is a silver star. It's a solid and surprisingly heavy little thing, with gently curved points. Holding it in my hand, I continue to read.

Nobody knows what happens to us when we die, Kitty, which is good, in a way, as it can be anything I want it to be in my mind. I like to think that sometimes I'll be able to look down and see you. Not all the time, because that would be intrusive, and there are some things a mother clearly does not want to see! But at the right times, those moments when you're walking along the street, or sitting at your desk, or laughing with your friends, or holding your own baby in your arms, those days I might be able to see you. Some of the big moments and lots of the little everyday ones. When I picture this, I think of sitting on a star, dangling my bare feet, and I'm so full of love that I swear you will be able to feel it shining down on you.

Do you know that the farthest star we can see with the naked eye is in a constellation called Cassiopeia? Please have a look for it on a clear night. It is 16,308 light-years away. I've never really understood light-years, even though Dad has been trying to explain them to me. He tells me that light can travel about six trillion miles in one year, and that's how it's calculated. You probably already knew that, but if not, ask Dad about it.

One thing I know for sure is that I have trillions of light-years of love for you that can never stop shining. Remember, even when you can't see the stars, even during the daytime when it seems as if they've gone away, they haven't, they're still there, shining down on you.

I love you to the moon and stars and back again.

Mum xxx

I put down the letter and let out a huge breath that I didn't even know I'd been holding. I can feel my heart pounding like an over-wound clock, but I can't hear anything, no birdsong, no lawn mower droning in the distance, not even the leaves of the great willow tree, which are shifting in the breeze. I wonder how much time has passed since I started reading the letter. It feels like hours, and I'm surprised to see it's still daylight rather than dusk. How strange that the thing I was most worried about turned out not to be true at all. Mum sounds exactly the same in her letter. She was as real to me as if she were sitting next to me, right here under this tree, smiling as she tucked my hair behind my ears and telling me to go and look up the word *maudlin* in a real dictionary and not on a phone.

Mum was big on vocabulary. She was passionate about words: reading, writing, crossword puzzles, Scrabble marathons, songs, poems, books, and plays. She inhaled words the way that I breathe in colors. Imogen and I have always had advanced vocabularies, but we learned so many new words over the last twelve months. Words that no child should ever have to learn, not in the way that we did, when they're happening to someone you love more than anything. Words like palliative care, metastasize, malignant, and pleural effusion; the vocabulary of cancer became part of our lives.

I wipe the tears from my eyes and reread the letter until I know it word for word. Then I don't know what to do, so I add the star to the charm bracelet, where it nestles against the heart. I lie back, the letter on my chest, and hold up my arm to watch the bracelet with its two dangling charms. At least that heart has company now.

CHAPTER THIRTEEN

EXCESS BAGGAGE

O ver the next few weeks, I carefully open and reread the letter dozens of times. Then I start to worry that I should limit my reading to once a week. What if all the folding and unfolding weakens the paper or the light fades the ink, or I get tears or snot on it? This letter needs looking after, like an ancient Egyptian manuscript or the Magna Carta. I go online and research archiving and preservation of valuable papers. Even though my letter is only a few weeks old, it's priceless and, as Gran always says, prevention is better than cure. Kate offered to make photocopies, but I don't like that idea. I find some crystal-clear archival bags, as used by the British Museum, and a collector grade three-ring binder, which costs thirty pounds. The Archival Preservation Society specifically cautions against confusing their superior products with those "inexpensive vinyl-clad school binders, which may cause image transfer and acid migration." Dad says a standard binder will be just fine, but I show him the website, and he studies it and my concerned face before agreeing to buy the collector's folder and the archival bags for Imogen and me.

At first, Imogen had laughed when I told her about my document preservation research, but she and I spend a pleasant Saturday afternoon together decorating our folders. She covers hers with pictures of things Mum loved: peonies, Dartmoor ponies, books, David Bowie, Bamburgh Beach, sandpiper birds, and photos of us. I cover mine with a rainbow of her favorite Farrow & Ball colors: Lulworth Blue, Wevet, Peignoir, Dimpse, Mizzle, and Mole's Breath. Mizzle, color 266, is a lovely made-up word to describe the color of the sky when there's mist and drizzle—it's mizzling.

As Imogen hasn't had a birthday since Mum died, she doesn't have a letter to put in her binder yet, which makes me feel secretly superior. I'm a bit ashamed of feeling that way, so I tell her that she can read my letter as often as she likes, as long as she asks me first and never takes it out of the archival bag.

And just like that, it's the last day of term. If we were in New York, we would have finished school in June. I can't believe how long the school summer holidays are in America. What I really can't believe is that I won't be sitting next to Jessica in September. We've been best friends since we met at age four at our "interview" for Haverstock Girls' School. She let me try on a princess dress she'd found in the dressing-up box, and I shared my snack with her. A teacher asked us each to say a rhyme we knew. We were supposed to recite "Twinkle, Twinkle," or "The Itsy-Bitsy Spider," but I said "cat and hat," and two girls laughed at me. Jess shoved them during playtime.

Imogen and I each have to go and see Mrs. Brooks on our last day. Imogen says it's like having to meet with the prison governor before they'll release you.

"We will miss you next term, Kitty, but I look forward to welcoming you back in January. It's a marvelous opportunity to spend time living overseas. As we say here at Haverstock Girls' School, 'Non sibi sed toti.' Not for self but for all. Inspiring words, I'm sure you'll agree, and words you will carry with you during your months in New York. Does your new school have a motto, dear?"

"Care, connect, compassion," I say.

"Oh, how lovely." She doesn't look impressed. "Shouldn't that be 'caring, connection, and compassion'? Well, never mind. I'm sure it is a wonderful school. Good luck, Kitty."

She pulls me into a warm hug, and I'm taken back in time to the day we returned to school after Mum died. I was surprised then by how soft and comforting it felt to hug her, and I'm surprised all over again.

I've decided to take as little as possible with me to New York, limiting my packing to a few books, photos, my color charts, stuffed animals, and some clothes. Since I've worn a school uniform five days a week for the last six years, I don't have many clothes, although weirdly, Imogen's wardrobe is overflowing. Twinkle, my tattered stuffed cat, will be traveling in my carry-on bag. Kate gave her to me when she came to visit me in the hospital on the day I was born. Twinkle was my first and best present. We've been through a lot together, and I wouldn't dream of putting her in the hands of careless baggage handlers and on conveyor belts that could malfunction. I've thrown up on Twinkle quite a few times over the years, and Dad said we should throw her away, but Mum always came to her rescue. She would put Twinkle on a delicates cycle in the washing machine before lovingly perching her on the radiator to dry. I would sit anxiously watching Twinkle's cream body tumble around inside the machine, her sweet upside-down face appearing at the washing machine window every so often. One of Twinkle's glassy green eyes has fallen off, and her cream fur is matted, but I wouldn't change her for the world. I'd contemplated making her a patch when her eye fell off. She'd look like a sweet four-legged pirate.

"Where are all your clothes, Kitty?" says Imogen, interrupting my mental patch design by rummaging around in my suitcase. "And why are you bringing five stuffed animals? Isn't stupid Twinkle enough?"

A few years ago Imogen had taken Twinkle and hidden her from me for hours. I've never seen Mum angrier with her.

"Get out of my case," I say, shoving her to one side.

I sneak into Imogen's room later to look in her bags. Under layers and layers of clothes, makeup, and framed photos of her and Josh, I find her ratty old purple poodle called Fifi, which she's had forever. Imogen isn't as cool as she likes to think she is. I smile as I carefully cover Fifi with T-shirts and jeans.

The house seems oddly quiet without Cleo, who moved to Gran's house the day after my birthday so that we could see her get settled into her temporary home. Who'd have thought that a small cat's absence would leave such a big gap? Gran and Cleo seem to be getting on quite well together, considering Gran doesn't really like cats, although she has threatened to ban Cleo from the living room for scratching the furniture.

"I don't want that cat going upstairs either, Kitty. You've spoiled her by letting her sleep on your bed. Now she expects me to do the same and completely ignores the lovely bed I bought her from the pet store. I wonder if I can return it. It cost twenty-five pounds. Also, she mews outside my bedroom door all night, and I can hear her, even with my earplugs in. Infuriating animal."

"Good girl, Cleo," I whisper into her silky black fur. "Just keep doing what you're doing, and she'll let you in eventually." Cleo gives a knowing little meow in reply. I bet that by the end of the month, Cleo will be sleeping on Gran's bed.

"I wish you were coming with us, Gran."

"I'm far too old to be gallivanting off to New York, Kitty. I'll be fine here, and I'll come and visit you soon. Anyway, before you know it, you'll be back here with me."

I stroke the back of her hand, which seems more dry and papery than I remember it feeling. The veins are navy blue and raised against her skin. The plain gold wedding band, which is the only jewelry I've ever seen her wear, is surprisingly shiny though.

"I'll miss you, Gran."

"I'll miss you too, darling."

We sit like that on the couch, Cleo on my lap and me resting my head on Gran's shoulder, until the sun dips, the room darkens, and Gran gets up to turn on the lamps.

During my last visit to Sam, he gives me the contact details for a therapist in New York City named Dr. Natasha Feld.

"Just in case you feel like talking to someone while you're away, Kitty. All true New Yorkers have a therapist. It would almost be weird not to." He grins. "I haven't met her, but one of my colleagues was at college with her. He says she's great. So how are the preparations for your move to the Big Apple? All packed?"

"Imogen and Dad are so excited about going. It's annoying."

"Why is it annoying?"

"It's like they're ready to move on. We shouldn't be moving on. We should be staying put."

"You need to allow yourself to be happy, Kitty. Laura used to say that happiness is the greatest gift a person could give. Your dad is trying to give all of you that gift. You should give yourself permission to accept it."

That sounds like something Mum would say. I don't speak and just stare at him instead. I've tried this type of conversational standoff with Sam a couple of times before, but I've always talked first. Well, not today. As if he knows that I'm not budging, Sam continues,

"Your grief is the natural counterpoint to your love, but there is real joy in living, Kitty, and your mum would want you to seize it with both hands."

"I don't want to be joyful," I say.

"That's understandable, but someday you will. Grief doesn't follow a set pattern, and it's different for everyone. It can come and go, hitting you between the eyes when you least expect it. You just need to let it be."

"This isn't making me feel better," I tell him.

"I'm not here to make you feel better, Kitty. Remember, we talked about that. I'm here to bear witness to your pain and to help explain the journey you are on when I can."

"Sam, can you do me a favor and go and visit Gran while I'm in New York? Please check on her once a week. I'm worried about her being lonely, even though she won't admit it. Kate's said she'd go to see her, and I'm going to ask Mrs. Allison as well."

Sam promises he will, and that evening I enlist Mrs. Allison.

"I know that Gran seems tough, but she isn't really," I say, unsure of how Mrs. Allison will respond to my request.

"Oh, I know. Eleanor's softer than she would like me to think," says Mrs. Allison. "Don't you worry, Kitty, dear, I've already got plans to invite her to Zumba. Also, the vicar told me about a new club they're starting at the church called Aging with Attitude. Doesn't that sound fun?"

"I guess," I say doubtfully. "Maybe you could go on an outing together? She likes the theater."

"Excellent idea, Kitty. I'll get us tickets for *Mamma Mia!* as a surprise. Everyone loves ABBA, don't they? It's a shame that Pierce Brosnan won't be in it. He was gorgeous in the film."

I was thinking more of a Shakespeare play at the Globe theater. I don't think Gran loves ABBA or Pierce Brosnan, whoever he is.

I can't get to sleep on our last night in London. I miss Cleo, who should be curled in the crook of my legs, and my bed feels empty without the stuffed animals, who are already packed in my suitcase downstairs waiting by the front door. Only trusty Twinkle is still with me. I think of the hundreds of nights I've slept in this bed and all the mornings waking up in it. Tomorrow will be my last waking up in my own bed for months. The pillow I'm lying on is the one I cried into when Mum got ill, and the one I used to battle Imogen with during our frequent pillow fights. I can picture Mum sitting on this bed reading to me and then singing me my favorite bedtime song that she made up for me, her voice like a hug.

My sweet Kitty, it's time that you sleep tight
Wrapped in lots of love just like every single night
So lovely Kitty, have the sweetest dreams
Wake up in the morning to the golden sunbeams
Until then Kitty, close your pretty eyes
I'll see you in the morning under bright blue skies

CHAPTER FOURTEEN

LADY LIBERTY GREEN

"Start spreading the news. I'm leaving today, I want to be a part of it, New York, New York."

"Dad, please stop. People are staring."

The other passengers on the 9:32 a.m. Heathrow Express are looking at my father with expressions ranging from bemused to amused. One businessman seems positively angry and mutters into his cell phone about "some bloody idiot singing on the train."

"We should have traveled by boat," Dad says, thawing the man's frosty glare with a smile and a nod. "How cool would it be to sail into New York Harbor under the watchful gaze of Lady Liberty? We'll have to go and visit her tomorrow. I have a brilliant first day planned for us. The Statue of Liberty was one of your mum's favorite things in New York. Kate said she has some lovely photos of Mum in front of it just after they graduated from university."

In spite of myself, I am excited to see New York. Fueled by books, images of the city are imprinted into my mind. From *Eloise* to *Tales of a Fourth Grade Nothing* via *Harriet the Spy*, no other city has loomed so large in my imagination, but arriving at John F. Kennedy Airport is a disappointingly unglamorous first experience of the city that never sleeps. The beigey-gray walls and grubby-looking carpet are at odds with my mental image of the gateway to New York City. I wonder if Dad has noticed the walls are the same color as pigeons. I had pictured JFK to look more like a nightclub, with flashing lights, velvet sofas, and sumptuous carpets that would cushion your every step. They could at least play Jay-Z over the speakers for ambiance, or Frank Sinatra for the old people.

"What is the reason for your visit, sir?" asks the terrifying-looking agent staring at us suspiciously as he examines our passports and Dad's visa.

"I'm here with my family on a temporary work assignment."

"And how long do you intend to stay in the United States?"

"Just until the end of the year." Dad smiles winningly.

The agent looks at the three of us with disapproval

and stamps our passports in silence, eventually returning them to Dad with a small nod. We walk away to
collect our suitcases, feeling bizarrely guilty.

The bags take ages to arrive. To pass the time, I
watch a friendly-looking beagle accompanied by an
unfriendly-looking police officer making the rounds
of the arrivals area. The dog is wearing a jacket with
a small American flag on it that says "K9 Protecting
America."

"He's looking for drug smugglers," says Imogen, "or
bombs."

The dog, who must have heard my idiotic sister say
two of his trigger words, makes a beeline for us, wagging
his tail. He starts to sniff my purple flowery backpack.

"Do you have any fruit in your bag, miss?" asks the
officer, who I'm sure has a gun on his belt, or is it called
a holster?

"Fruit?" I ask as the dog stares at my bag. If he could
point his paw, he probably would. "Why, does your dog
like fruit?"

"Bringing fruit or vegetables into the United States is
prohibited," says the officer sternly.

I start to ask him why on earth it's illegal to bring a
cucumber or a pear into America, but Dad nudges me
and opens my bag. The officer removes books, headphones, Twinkle, a pencil case, my diary, and there, at

the very bottom of my backpack, is an apple. The dog wags his tail smugly, and the officer gives him a treat and points at the nearest trash can, where I drop the apple in shame. We've attracted quite a crowd with this little sideshow, and I notice a couple of other British tourists scrabbling around in their bags before discreetly disposing of bananas and other fruit contraband.

"I think they should have arrested you, Kitty," says Imogen as we wheel our bags outside. "Made an example of you for trying to smuggle illegal goods into the United States."

Imogen is every bit as annoying in New York as she was in London.

When we walk out of the terminal building we're smacked in the face by a wall of heat and humidity. Welcome to New York in August. We join the long line of travelers waiting for a yellow cab, and I feel a sudden pang for the friendly black cabs of London. By the time we get to the front of the queue, we're all pink and damp, especially me. Our T-shirts are glued to our backs. Even my ordinarily fragrant-looking sister is sweating rather than glowing.

The taxi ride from the airport into Manhattan is hideous. The cab driver veers wildly across lanes without checking in his mirror first. Perhaps he prefers not to know if he is seconds from death. I can guarantee that I am seconds from vomiting in the back seat.

"They don't seem to do mirror, signal, maneuver in this country, do they?" says Dad through gritted teeth as we make another deranged three-lane traverse. The driver's latest antics are heralded with a fanfare of horns and rude hand gestures from other drivers.

"Can you slow down a bit, mate?" asks Dad. The cab driver responds by swerving violently to the left.

"Dad, I think I'm going to be sick," I say.

"It's okay, love. We'll be there soon. Let me open the window and get you some fresh air." Dad winds down the window, and the cab is filled with a blast of steamy August air.

"Dad, can we have the window closed? It's messing up my hair. Kitty's fine."

"Please leave it, Dad. I really think I might throw up!"

"Imogen, the window is staying open. Kitty is clearly unwell. Don't worry about your hair."

The cab driver seems to have worked off whatever anger he had toward the traffic or life in general and begins driving much more calmly. Either that or he heard me say I was about to throw up and decided it was better to slow down rather than spend twenty minutes trying to clean up an English girl's barf.

"Wow!" says Imogen, and I lean over Dad to look out of her window. Unfolding beside us like the Emerald City appearing at the end of the Yellow Brick Road is the Manhattan skyline in all its glory. It's backlit by gold in the afternoon sunlight and looks impossibly small, like an intricate model inside a snow globe. I want to pick it up and shake it. The whole place glows.

"Eight million people live in New York City," says Dad. "Isn't it amazing, girls?"

"It's beautiful," we chorus and the three of us grin at each other and squeeze hands. The hot air is turning the back of the cab into a steam room, so now that I don't feel like barfing, I close the window.

"Welcome to New York!" says the cab driver, breaking his silence of the last ninety minutes and turning around in his seat to beam at us.

"Please face the front," Dad says.

We drive across the Brooklyn Bridge to enter Manhattan. On the left-hand side, standing majestically in New York Harbor, as if she's been waiting there all this time just to greet us, is the Statue of Liberty. She's smaller than I'd expected and a beautiful green, which would make an excellent addition to the Farrow & Ball palette. I can imagine the description on the website—"this exquisite shade of green is reminiscent of the oxidized copper of New York's iconic statue. Lady Liberty Green sits happily in both contemporary settings and period homes and is ideal for use in entrance halls and dining rooms."

Driving through the streets of the city is like being in a film. There are hot dog stands on each corner and a constant surge of people wherever I look. Throbbing music comes from somewhere, and the streets are pulsing. We drive across a highway, a game of baseball improbably taking place between skyscrapers, the Freedom Tower looming in the background, and pull up outside a tall apartment building. So this is where I'll be living. I step out of the car and am back in the sauna. I swear the air even tastes hot. Because we are by the river, it's breezier, but rather than being refreshing, it's as if someone is pointing a hair dryer at my face. We go through the revolving doors into a pristine marble lobby and are immediately plunged into an icebox of air-conditioning. It's a relief for precisely a minute, and then I start getting goose bumps on my arms and have to rummage through my bag for my sweatshirt. These extreme swings in temperature are definitely going to make me ill.

A friendly-looking doorman welcomes us to the building and hands Dad a manila envelope with the keys to our new apartment. My ears pop on the way to the twenty-fourth floor, likely the combination of the plane ride and this speedy elevator, but when we walk into the apartment, it's my eyes that pop at the view. There's a wall of six oversize windows, which look out onto the Hudson River and a park below. The park has a circular lawn busy with New Yorkers sunbathing, playing Frisbee, walking dogs, picnicking, and running. Why would anyone choose to run in this heat?

I peer down nervously, and my stomach lurches. I'm relieved when Dad takes one look at my face and tells me that there are child locks on the windows, and they will only open a tiny bit. It's not that I'm scared of heights exactly, but I often have an urge to throw something off a balcony or over the side of a bridge. On a family day out to visit the Tower of London a few years ago, Mum told us that it's called the "high place phenomenon" and is perfectly normal.

"It doesn't sound perfectly normal," said Dad, eyeing me as I clutched my backpack on Tower Bridge.

Mum gently removed it from my hands.

"Well, it is. Edgar Allan Poe even wrote a short story about it called "The Imp of the Perverse." It's the same compulsion that makes people want to shout out in the quiet parts of a church service."

"Edgar Allan Poe was a complete freak who died of rabies," said Imogen. "We studied him in English last term and voted him the poet most likely to have been a serial killer."

Mum ignored these fascinating facts and gave me a comforting pat on the shoulder.

"As the only one here with any medical qualifications, I can assure you, Kitty, that it is perfectly normal. I even have it myself sometimes." She smiled at me and passed the bag to Dad.

"Either that or it's a good excuse not to have to carry anything when we cross a bridge," Dad said. "Remind me never to book a family trip to Venice."

The living room, dining room, and kitchen are all one open space. To the left of the front door is Dad's bedroom, which has a tiny en suite bathroom, and to the right are two identical small bedrooms joined by what, according to Dad, is called a Jack and Jill bathroom.

"Or in this case, Jill and Jill," he says, clearly pleased with this comedy comment.

All the walls are painted a flat white, and the furniture is white, cream, and light wood. Even the floorboards are pale, and I think with a pang of the rich mahogany antique boards at home, the floor made even brighter by vibrantly colored Turkish rugs in inky blues and ruby reds. This place urgently needs an injection of color. I flick through my mental paint chart and think about the colors I would use to make this feel like a home.

Parma Gray, color 27, would add dimension and softness to the living room. I would use Pavilion Blue, color 252, in Dad's room, the same greeny-blue of the Royal Pavilion in Brighton, where Dad proposed to Mum. For Imogen's room, Sulking Room Pink, 295, how appropriate. It's called Sulking Room Pink because the French used that shade in boudoirs, and the word *bouder* means to sulk. Oh, the things you can learn from imaginatively named paint. For my room, I'll use Setting Plaster, color number 231, a dusty pink so pale it looks as if the walls are delicately blushing.

Standing in this white box, with all of Manhattan spread out in front of me, I'm surprised to feel a little color trickle back into my life, and I give a shiver of excitement, this one not caused by the arctic air-conditioning. Perhaps coming to New York wasn't the worst idea Dad ever had. I guess I'll find out soon enough.

CHAPTER FIFTEEN

LOST IN TRANSLATION

We spend our first week in New York doing all the usual touristy things. We visit Central Park, the Empire State Building, Times Square, the High Line, and Wall Street. We take a tour bus and ride past the famous sights of the city. The Chrysler Building is my favorite, Imogen adores the Flatiron Building, and we both love the Plaza Hotel, where our childhood heroine Eloise used to run wild. After reading that book, Imogen was desperate to go and live at the Ritz. I've seen all of these things before in films or books, but nobody had told me about the steam that rises unexpectedly from the street, making everything smell like laundry for a split second. It's enchanting, although the smell of pee that sometimes lingers outside subway stations is less so. The hundreds of yellow cabs and the endless honking of horns just add to the New Yorkiness of it all. The sun shines brightly every day, displayed to perfection in a brilliant blue sky, St Giles Blue, color number 280, to be precise. London's summer sky is a gentle Blue Ground, color number 210, but in New York, the sky demands your attention. It yells, "Hey you, look up, look at me, now!" so you lift your head obediently, the skyscrapers make your head spin and your tummy lurch, and then there it is, the bluest of blue skies.

We take a boat to see the Statue of Liberty up close and climb the 377 steps to stand in her crown. While everyone else is gazing out at the stunning views of the harbor and city blanketed below us, I look up and see the wavy lines of Lady Liberty's hair. Back on board, there's a welcome breeze from the relentlessly sunny weather. Imogen's ponytail whips my face as we lean over the railing of the boat to cool off. After a few days exploring the city, we look as if we've spent a week on the beach in Greece. Imogen is a lovely honey color and some of my freckles have joined together. Dad has lost the ghostly pallor I'd become accustomed to over the last six months. We get off the boat again at Ellis Island, which is where all immigrants arriving in New York used to land. The guide informs us that twelve million settlers were processed here from 1892 to 1954 and that despite sometimes being referred to as the Island of Tears, the majority of immigrants were well treated.

"It looks better than JFK," I whisper to Dad, obviously not quietly enough since the tour guide chuckles and tells me I should try landing at LaGuardia Airport if I think JFK's bad.

There are hundreds of pictures of immigrants. Imogen finds a photo of a twelve-year-old Polish girl with sad eyes who she says looks like me. I try to find a picture of someone who resembles Imogen, but she informs me that she would have been traveling first class, so she wouldn't have had to go through Ellis Island. The girl in the sepia photo is wearing a scratchy-looking wool shawl around her shoulders, and a scarf covers most of her hair. I wonder what her name was, where her parents were, and what became of her. Dad eventually nudges me along to look at the rest of the exhibition, but I can't stop thinking about my sad-eyed Polish look-alike. I hope she had a happy life in New York.

In the evenings before school starts, we travel the world through New York's restaurants. We go to Little Italy for pizza, eat at Greek restaurants in Astoria, and gobble Puerto Rican food in Harlem. Dad lets us order breakfast for dinner at a diner in SoHo, which has turquoise plastic seats and ridiculously tall stacks of pancakes. Dad excitedly requests his eggs sunny-side up, and I have mine over easy. Cooking styles for eggs in America sound so much more fun than in England.

The waistband on my shorts is starting to dig into my skin, leaving an angry red button-and-zipper-shaped indent on my stomach. Some evenings we have food delivered to the apartment; the doorman always calls us to let us know that a delivery is on its way up to us. We order Chinese food and are thrilled by the little white rice containers, chopsticks, and fortune cookies that are delivered.

"It's just like in *Friends*," says Imogen as she unpacks the cartons of food. She's been binge-watching the series on Netflix ever since Dad mentioned moving to New York. She snaps open her cookie, smiles, and reads, "'Your success will astonish those around you.' Well, I don't think anyone will be surprised by my success. What does yours say, Kitty?"

"'The usefulness of a cup is in its emptiness.' What does that even mean? How is that a fortune? 'Lucky numbers: 13, 16, 47, 28, 54, 9.' Dad, what does yours say?"

"Your daughters will load the dishwasher."

He's quite the comedian these days. I'm so pleased to hear him make jokes again that I laugh as if it's one of the funniest things I've ever heard, while Imogen groans and rolls her eyes.

We shop in small bodegas and a giant Whole Foods bursting with gorgeous-looking organic fruit and vegetables, artisanal bread, kombucha, cold-brewed coffee, and thirty-two varieties of granola—I know because I counted them.

"It's so much more glamorous than Waitrose," Imogen says, loading the cart with green smoothies, pineapples, and kale. She's doing a cleanse called the Glow-Up Challenge, which she will immortalize on Instagram to share with her 1,862 followers. Dad and I ate hot dogs earlier in the week that we'd bought from a vendor in Central Park. It seemed a very New Yorky thing to do, but my stomach felt a bit funny afterward, so Imogen was probably right not to join us.

As the last days of August fade away and the start of school looms, I begin to feel nervous and lose my appetite. Even the delicious pancakes at the diner aren't tempting anymore. Dad tries to reassure me that it will be great, but what does he know about American schools? By the time Labor Day comes around, I am a nervous wreck. Labor Day is the Monday before school starts and the official end of the summer. According to the local news, nobody should be wearing white after today.

"That's ridiculous," says Imogen. "It's like a hundred degrees outside. How can it be the end of summer?"

Apparently, the no-white rule is in place until

Memorial Day. I have absolutely no idea when Memorial Day is.

Imogen and I have been discussing whether we'll get marked down for using English spellings in our schoolwork.

"That would be so unfair," I say. "The subject is English, not American. *Labour* has a letter *u* in it, *maths* is plural since it's short for mathematics, and zed is the last letter of the alphabet, not zee."

"Chill out, Kitty. You're fulfilling every stereotype of a stuck-up Brit! When in Rome and all that."

Annoyingly, Imogen has started calling things by their American names and keeps saying sidewalk, sneakers, elevator, and most irritatingly of all, pants instead of trousers. She loves shouting, "Check out my pants!" which isn't nearly as funny as she thinks it is. If Imogen lived in Rome, she would say she lived in Roma. My sister's right, though—people are going to think I'm stuck up. The more nervous I get, the more stilted my accent becomes. As Imogen begins to elongate her vowels, I clip mine back to compensate. Dad points out that I'm starting to sound like the queen or someone from one of those black-and-white films about the Second World War.

"Brits and Americans, separated by a common

language," says Dad. "A guy at work sent a hilarious email the other day to welcome me to the office, with a list of commonly misunderstood expressions. When an English person says 'That's very interesting,' they mean 'What utter drivel'; 'quite good' translates to 'bloody awful'; and 'I'll bear that in mind' means 'I've already forgotten whatever nonsense you just spouted.'"

Half of New York seems to be going back-to-school shopping. The streets of SoHo are packed, and Staples, where we go to get folders, pencils, and paper, looks like it's been raided by marauding Vikings—not that Alfhild's family would ever have done anything like that. We buy jeans from Levi's, T-shirts, shorts, and leggings from H&M and Brandy Melville, backpacks from a place called Fjällräven, and shoes from Adidas. It's weird to be buying running shoes to wear to school instead of the regulation black, brown, or navy flats I'm used to wearing.

As we traipse into yet another store, Dad sighs, clearly finding a marathon shopping trip with his daughters in one-hundred-degree heat draining. He must have lost the ability to think clearly as Imogen manages to convince him to buy her expensive running shorts for gym class from Lululemon, and he nearly faints as he hands over his credit card.

"Seventy-two dollars for a pair of shorts," he splutters. "They're fourteen pounds in Marks & Spencer for a pack of two."

Imogen totes the chic red-and-black Lululemon bag containing the single pair of shorts while I lug the Brandy Melville, H&M, and Levi's bags. Dad struggles with the rest of the shopping through crowds of people— they all seem to be walking in the opposite direction to us. He stops apologizing for hitting people with the enormous Staples bag when he realizes that most of them are, in fact, walking directly into him. Imogen's bag has cutesy sayings written on it like "Dance, sing, floss, and travel" and "Friends are more important than money."

"Not if you want to shop at Lululemon they're not," Dad mutters and makes Imogen carry the Staples bag as well.

When we get home, Imogen and I spend an unusually companionable couple of hours trying on potential first-day of school outfits while Dad has a lie-down with a cold washcloth on his face. It wasn't that bad! We parade through the Jack and Jill bathroom modeling our new looks.

"It's so hot, I really want to wear the shorts tomorrow," says Imogen, who is looking gorgeous in denim shorts with a navy-and-white striped T-shirt. We both seem to have purchased quite a lot of navy blue, perhaps an unconscious homage to our school in London. "But what if nobody else is wearing shorts? It would be so embarrassing if I were the only one. I don't even know if we're allowed to wear them. There has to be some type of dress code. I'm going to check the website. I wish I knew someone who goes there so I could ask."

My sister sounds almost nervous. Maybe she doesn't take everything in her gazelle-like stride after all. It could be that beneath her glossy exterior is an anxious girl who's as worried as I am about fitting in at her new school. I imagine Imogen as Ponytail Girl, finally revealing a chink in her armor to her trusty sidekick, aka me. I really need to think up a good superhero name for myself. Anyway, Ponytail Girl showing a bit of vulnerability will make her more relatable—even if she can grow a waist-length ponytail in seconds and shoot scrunchies from her wrists. I decide to go and write this scene in my book, *The Swishes of Ponytail Girl*. The story is coming along well, although without the pictures, it's not nearly as good as it should be. I wish for the thousandth time that I could draw or paint something apart from walls— then I'd have somewhere for all the colors in my head to land instead of them swirling around inside me.

We decide to FaceTime Gran before it gets too late to call England. It's strange to sit here in New York with the sun blazing in through the windows and the air-conditioning blasting out while Gran is dressed for bed in her flannel robe. She tells us that she had to put the heat on, since there's been a cold snap in London. We gave Gran a new computer so that she could email and FaceTime us while we're away. We made her promise to hold Cleo up to the camera and to let Mrs. Allison use the computer sometimes, because she doesn't have one. Mrs. Allison said she doesn't trust computers.

"I read somewhere that criminals can watch you through that little camera at the top of the screen. Russian and Chinese spies!" she told Dad in a stage whisper as he tried to explain FaceTime.

"Let me guess, Elizabeth," said Gran. "You read that in the *Daily Mail*."

"I put a sliding cover over the lens," said Dad, trying to keep the peace, "Even Mark Zuckerberg has one. Just remember to slide it back before you call us so that we can see you."

"I've no idea who Mark Zuckwhatever is, but perhaps he read the same article as I did, which was indeed in the *Daily Mail*, thank you, Eleanor."

"Well, you have to move with the times," said Gran smugly. "The rate of progress these days is extraordinary."

"It's not what I'd call extraordinary," Mrs. Allison

replied. "They said we'd have flying cars by now, and do we have any? Not that I've noticed."

Gran lifts Cleo up to the camera. The cat immediately blocks the lens with her black furry face and proceeds to step on the keyboard, which disconnects us. When Gran calls back, Cleo is on the floor in disgrace. We give Gran a virtual tour of our new apartment. She's most impressed by the views of the river and the Jack and Jill bathroom, but sensibly points out that Imogen and I should probably have a pre-agreed morning schedule to avoid arguments.

"So that would be Imogen from 6:45 to 7:15 and Kitty from 7:15 to 7:18," Imogen laughs.

"Actually, I need at least five minutes, dummy," I say.

"Are you excited about school, Kitty?" Gran asks.

"Nervous. I can't stop thinking about Jess and everyone else going back to school in London. I even miss the uniform. Having to decide what you're going to wear each day is exhausting. What have you been doing, Gran?"

"Well, I went to a Zumba class with Mrs. Allison this morning. It was extraordinary, and not in a good way. I won't be doing that again, but they do offer Pilates classes at the same studio, so we're going to give that a try on Wednesday. That seems more my type of thing. Kate came for a visit yesterday and took me out for a lovely lunch, so I've been keeping busy. I am tired, though, because I've had a few interrupted nights' sleep."

I must look worried—maybe Gran can't sleep because she's missing us too much. But she quickly explains that Cleo has learned how to open the door to her bedroom, so she's decided it's easier to let her stay in there. It looks like Cleo has claimed her rightful place within a couple of weeks, just as I predicted. Gran and I talk until Imogen kicks me off the laptop to have one of her marathon FaceTime calls with Josh. I told Dad I don't think she should be allowed to FaceTime her boyfriend from her bedroom. I said I thought it was inappropriate.

"Mind your own business, Kitty," Imogen said. "You're just jealous because you'll never have a boyfriend."

"Imogen, don't be mean," said Dad, ruffling my hair. "Kitty, you really should mind your own business."

I lie awake for ages worrying about school, and whether anyone will talk to me tomorrow. For the longest time, I've felt as though I've been underwater, but now I feel like I'm on the highest diving board at the pool. The one I would never jump off, but there's a long line of kids jostling impatiently behind me, and I'm going to have to jump because they won't let me go back down the ladder. I do some of the deep breathing exercises that Mum used to do with me when I couldn't sleep. She called it belly breathing, one hand on my chest, one on my stomach, breathe in for four and out for four. The hand on the chest should stay still, and the one on the belly should rise and fall. I belly breathe for about a hundred breaths, but even though I'm doing it right and my hand is rising and falling just as it should be, it's not helping, so I turn my lamp back on and read until I can feel my eyes closing. I summon up an image of Cleo, and eventually, the thought of a sweet little black cat on the other side of the Atlantic, with her tail curled neatly around her body, sleeping at the bottom of Gran's bed, lulls me to sleep.

CHAPTER SIXTEEN

THE BOY WITH THE BLUE HAIR

On the first day of school, Dad and I take a cab, although after today I'll be taking the subway with Imogen. Her school is a few stops after mine. She refused to let Dad go with her on her first day.

"Everyone would think I'm a complete loser. There is no way you are dropping me off at school. No way!"

There was no way I was turning up alone on my first day, so it worked out for everyone. The taxi stops in front of a new-looking redbrick building. The school is six stories high, with a minuscule playground on one side.

"There's another playground on the roof," says Dad. "How cool is that?"

"Is that safe?" I ask, images of balls and children flying off the roof whizzing through my mind.

"It's covered in net," Dad says.

"Like one of those covers that Mrs. Allison puts on

cakes in the summer to keep flies from getting to them?"

"I suppose so." Dad sighs, stops, and looks right at me. "I need you to be a bit more enthusiastic, please, Kitty. This is an excellent school. I know someone who sends their child here, and they love it."

The principal is standing at the entrance, welcoming back his students. He introduces himself as Principal Carter, and he and Dad shake hands vigorously. He is very casually dressed for a principal, not even wearing a jacket or tie. The kids crowding the hallways are a blur of color and noise. I see children sporting hoodies and leggings, and one boy wearing what looks like a panda onesie. A little girl walks by wearing a pair of cat ears on a headband and meows at us. The principal actually meows back! A boy with blue hair wanders past, headphones on ears.

"Morning, Henry," says Principal Carter. "No headphones in school, please."

The boy shrugs, smiles, and pushes the headphones down to his shoulders. I'm frankly surprised headphones are banned given the panda onesie, the cat ears, and the mewing.

"Henry, meet Kitty. She'll be joining your class. Please show her to the seventh-grade classroom and introduce her to Ms. Lyons." Principal Carter smiles kindly at me. "Have an excellent first day, Kitty."

The seventh-grade classroom is noisy and fizzing with the energy and excitement of what seems like fifty kids but is probably only half that number. Henry delivers me to Ms. Lyons and strolls off to a desk at the back of the room.

"You must be Kitty," Ms. Lyons says, smiling. "Come and have a seat next to Ava. She'll be showing you around today."

Ava gives me a dazzling smile, and I blink at the whiteness of her teeth and the coolness of her outfit. She's wearing black jeans, a gray T-shirt that says ICON on it in big red letters, and enormous gold hoop earrings. I touch my unpierced earlobe. I wonder if Dad will take me to get mine done this weekend.

"Hi!" Ava says. "You're from London, right? I love it there. I went last summer with my parents. Do you love New York? Have you been here before? Which city do you prefer? I love Rome too, do you?"

I discover later that firing off questions without waiting for an answer is one of Ava's habits.

"Okay, thank you, Ava. Take a breath. There will be plenty of time to tell Kitty about your travels at recess," Ms. Lyons says.

The first class of the day is something called ethics. Is that even a subject? I was hoping for English or art. I decide to keep quiet and listen to the other kids.

"To start off the school year we'll be discussing the moral compass and how we define it," says Ms. Lyons. "Anyone care to share their thoughts? What constitutes unethical behavior?"

"I lied to my parents last night about finishing my summer homework," calls out a boy, without bothering to raise his hand. "I hadn't, but I wanted to play video games. Anyway, that's the most unethical thing I did this week, so far at least."

A bunch of kids snicker. The teacher thanks him for his honesty and suggests he use the time at recess to finish his homework. My jaw is dropping for three reasons: (1) how is this boy not in trouble, (2) why on earth did he just confess that in a lesson, and (3) we had summer homework? While I'm pondering these questions, a girl starts giving an impassioned speech about the ethics of universal healthcare.

"Like your National Health Service, Kitty," says the teacher. "Perhaps you could tell us about that in a future class."

I don't think the class wants to hear about my experiences with the NHS. I had my appendix successfully removed when I was nine, but then at age ten, I watched as doctors and nurses tried and failed to cure my mum.

* * *

Perhaps it's the presence of boys at the school, but the noise level during recess is deafening. Basketballs fly around, prevented from raining down on the unsuspecting pedestrians below only by the giant net that covers the playground. I sit with Ava and a gaggle of other girls and try to remember to smile and look interested. They all seem much older than my classmates at home. I suppose I'm one of the youngest in seventh grade. I should be in sixth grade, but Mrs. Brooks said the work would be too easy for me. I don't think she considered the social side of things. Socially I should probably be in fourth grade. Fortunately, I don't need to say much since the girls maintain a constant stream of chatter among themselves about their summers, the teachers, clothes, camp, classmates, and how annoying their parents are.

By lunchtime, I'm wilting like a limp lettuce leaf. The effort of being friendly to people and trying to seem relaxed and vaguely cool has left me needing a nap. Why do people say a change is as good as a rest? Change is exhausting. I wonder how Imogen is getting on. She's probably already made loads of new friends and been voted Most Likely to Sail Through Life. I miss Jessica and start to feel the heat behind my eyes that's a sure indicator of impending tears, so I rub them roughly. Hopefully, people think I have allergies.

After lunch, I find myself sitting next to Henry, the

boy with the blue hair, for geography as the seat next to Ava has been taken by one of the giggly girls I'd met earlier. Henry doodles his way through the lesson, creating miracles in black ink on the front of his folder. His drawing is amazingly intricate, and I crane my neck to look at his picture of Spider-Man swinging from the Statue of Liberty's torch. He would be perfect to do the illustrations for the *Ponytail Girl* graphic novel. Henry notices me looking and turns the folder toward me to give me a better view. I give him a small smile and try to pay attention to the teacher, hoping to hide the fact that my US geography is terrible. I can't name all the states and know hardly any of their capitals. Why this is important, I have no idea. I've never been asked to name all the counties in England or their main towns. Bizarrely it turns out that the state capital of New York is a place called Albany. I've never even heard of Albany! Why on earth wouldn't New York be the state capital of New York? It makes zero sense. I feel like whispering this to Henry but stop myself. Does Imogen know the state capital is Albany? I make a mental note to ask her when I get home.

At the end of the day, Ava and I walk to the subway station together. We stop at Starbucks, and I'm impressed when she pulls out a credit card. She casually orders an iced Frappuccino with soy milk and extra caramel. I only ever order hot chocolate in Starbucks, so I say no to her offer of a drink, because I'm pretty sure ordering hot chocolate would be an NYC tween faux pas, and anyway, I don't have any money to pay her back. Dad was supposed to give me ten dollars for emergencies this morning but forgot. I never used to have emergency money for school in London. The fact that Dad thinks I might need it here makes me feel nervous about the journey home. While we're waiting for her drink to arrive, Ava gives me a summary of her eight years of experience of our classmates, which includes some eye-opening and, in some cases, eye-watering details.

"Who was the most annoying kid you met so far?" Ava asks.

"Everyone seemed fine."

"You're so polite, Kitty. You must not have met Max or any of his friends, then. They're total losers. Also, did you even speak to Lulu? She's a nightmare. She's the worst gossip, so don't tell her anything you don't want the whole school to know. What did you think of Henry?"

"Henry with the blue hair? He's okay. He didn't say much."

"He doesn't. If you get ten words out of him a week, he'll have been in a chatty mood. The blue hair's not bad. You should have seen it before the summer when it was orange. He changes it every few months."

Henry's hair is Hague Blue, color number 30, but I don't tell Ava that. It's way too early to talk about Farrow & Ball with Ava. She may, in fact, be the kind of person I can never talk to about my color charts.

"Henry's dad is James Davenport," Ava announces.

When I look at her blankly, she continues.

"Oh come on, Kitty, he's a famous actor! My mom has the biggest crush on him. I bet your mom will do morning drop-off for the rest of the year when you tell her that James Davenport is one of the dads at school. Was she at work this morning? Is that why your dad brought you in for your first day?"

Ava actually pauses for once and seems to be waiting for an answer to her last question. I look at my new Adidas shoes. This is an issue I hadn't even considered. Nobody here knows about Mum. Everyone in London knew, so I never needed to explain why she wasn't at a play, or parents' evening, or sports day.

"She couldn't come today," I say quietly.

"Well, tell her my mom will definitely be recruiting her for the PTA, and she won't take no for an answer. By the way, that's your platform," Ava says, waving her Frappuccino in the direction of a set of stairs. "I go uptown. See you tomorrow."

I walk down the stairs and can see Ava standing on the opposite platform. She waves her drink at me again, and I wave back, feeling foolish and wishing the train would arrive. When it does, I hop into the crowded car, thinking about what I had said. Why didn't I just tell Ava that Mum died? I mean, it wasn't a lie to say she couldn't drop me off at school, but it was definitely misleading. A lie by omission, Mum would have called it. How am I going to fix this?

I head to the apartment that's not home.

"How was your day, Imo?"

My sister walks in, dumps her bag on the table, and kicks her sneakers across the hallway.

"A freak spat on my new shoes on the subway," she says.

"Gross!"

"New York's full of weirdos. At least no one used the train as a toilet, not in my car, at least. Anyway, I'm chucking these shoes straight down the garbage chute. I texted Dad to ask him to pick up some new ones for me on his way home. He feels so bad about someone spitting at me that he's buying me the powder-blue pair as well, so that almost makes it worth it."

"Did anyone ask you about Mum, Imo?"

"Mum?" Imogen stops checking her phone and looks up at me. "No. Why would they?"

"A girl in my grade named Ava asked me. She wanted

to know why Mum hadn't brought me to school on my first day."

Imogen studies me carefully. "How very nosy of Ava. What did you tell her?"

"I sort of let her think Mum is still alive," I say miserably.

"What do you mean?"

"I said that Mum couldn't drop me off this morning," I groan, realizing how terrible that sounds.

"Ugh. How do you get yourself into these situations, Kitty? What are you going to do now?"

"I don't know. What do you think I should do?"

"I think you should stop being such a weirdo."

Even though Imogen's words are harsh, her voice is soft with sympathy, and her eyes are filled with concern. Suddenly the whole thing is too much: Imogen's uncharacteristic pity combined with the new school, the unfamiliar faces, the subway, and my conversation with Ava. I feel so alone. I wish we'd never come here, and I don't ever want to go back to that school. I burst into tears.

"It's okay, Kitty," says Imogen, pulling me into a rare hug. "It's not like this Ava girl's going to keep asking you. Next time it comes up, just say Mum died and leave it at that. She'll feel so sorry for you she won't mention it again."

Based on the little I know about Ava, I sincerely doubt she won't mention it again.

"Kitty, maybe you should tell Dad about what happened today." Imogen examines my face even more closely. "Or you could FaceTime Sam."

The thought of telling Sam about my conversation with Ava makes my cheeks burn. I can see his gentle, concerned face and hear his question: "What do you think made you say that, Kitty?" Talking to a new therapist seems like a complete waste of time, though. Dr. Natasha Feld, who Sam told me about, would be six months behind in the story. She's missed the most critical parts of the saddest book, the pages you absolutely have to read to understand and care about the characters. She can't skim read them now. It's too late. Dad will just be disappointed that I'm not processing things, not moving on like he wants me to so badly. I'll have to figure out a way to fix this myself, but right now all I want to do is go to sleep. I make Imogen promise not to say anything to Dad and head to my room. I wonder if it's possible that Ava will forget what I said. Maybe the problem will just disappear. Maybe the universe will finally take pity on me. Something inside tells me not to hold my breath.

CHAPTER SEVENTEEN

CHUTES AND LADDERS

The universe doesn't take pity on me—no change there then—and things get worse, not better, when Ava and I run into her mum at the end of the next day. Ava's mum is wearing workout clothes but looks immaculately made up, her hair blown out in a black sheet of perfection. She can't possibly have been exercising. When she hugs me, she's so waiflike I feel as if I should be lumbering around on a basketball court. The loudness of her voice takes me by surprise; it's such a stark contrast to her delicate appearance.

"You must be Kitty. It's so wonderful to have you here at the school. Did Ava tell you I used to work in London? Which neighborhood do you live in? We lived in Notting Hill. We just adore London. How are you enjoying school? Ava mentioned that your mom might be interested in joining the PTA. Do you think she would? We'd love to have her. I desperately need some help organizing the Halloween dance. Somehow I am always the one who ends up doing everything." Ava's mum sighs and closes her eyes as if she's doing some yoga breathing exercise. "Let her know my number is in the school directory, and I look forward to hearing from her. Make sure you tell her to call me, okay? Bye, girls!"

I look at Ava's mum, feeling like a whirlwind just hit me, a whirlwind that never took a breath, even when peppering me with questions. Now I know where Ava gets the machine-gun questioning style.

"Imagine what it's like living with her," Ava says, watching her mother disappear down the hallway, students and teachers alike stepping out of her determined path. "My dad says he hopes he loses his hearing when he gets old!"

Now would be a good time to tell Ava the truth, but hearing her mum talk about my mum joining a committee and helping to organize the school dance has made the lie seem much bigger. I scrunch my face up, trying to think of the right words.

"Um, Ava, I need to tell you . . ."

"Maddie!" she shrieks as her best friend appears from the gym. "Got to run, Kitty. See you tomorrow."

Ava swishes off down the hallway, a mini-me of her mum, and I stand there with my mouth open, the unspoken words stuck in my throat. Now what?

By the end of Friday, I still haven't told Ava the truth. Her mum cornered me again in the hallway, asking if I'd given my mum her message and why she couldn't find her contact details in the school directory. I stupidly answered that I didn't know why her number isn't there and wandered away, feeling ashamed. I'm so relieved that it's the weekend tomorrow and I'll be able to hide in my room for two days. Ava has her cello lesson after school, so I wander to the gates alone, shrugging my heavy backpack over one shoulder as all the other girls do. Apparently, it's not cool to wear both straps of your backpack. Imogen told me I looked like a hiker when I tried it on like that in the store. How does she know these magic rules? How does everyone seem to know the magic rules?

"Much better for your back to wear it that way," Dad had said. "Very sensible, Kitty." His words immediately convinced me to never again wear both straps.

As if I'd conjured him up, there's Dad standing at the gates deep in conversation with a petite woman wearing a stylish yoga outfit. Oh God, it's Ava's mum. She will have told Dad what I said or didn't say. Dad's eyes meet mine, but instead of looking angry, they're filled with love and concern. Ava's mum turns to follow his gaze, and when she sees me, her pointy features soften. She says something to Dad, hugs him, and walks briskly over, holding her arms out to me.

"I'm so sorry, Kitty." Ava's mum pulls me into a hug, squishing me against her bony frame. "I feel awful for hassling you this week about getting your mom's info. Your dad told me that you lost her in the spring."

I pull back out of her embrace, breathing hard. Lost is the worst euphemism for death imaginable. I hate it, and I hate Ava's mum for saying it. It makes it sound as if we'd carelessly misplaced Mum in the park. We didn't. She was taken from us. She was stolen, not lost. I glare at her and she takes a step back, alarmed by my angry gaze.

"Look, your dad's waiting for you." She shepherds me toward him. "Oh, and Kitty, I won't say anything to Ava. You can tell her about your mom in your own time."

At the end of a tear-filled weekend, I agree to FaceTime Sam. His familiar face appears on the computer, but he's not in his office; I suppose he doesn't usually work on a Sunday. The unfamiliar room must be his living room, I realize. I never thought of Sam having a home before. Like a teacher who you can't imagine existing outside the classroom, and you are shocked if you run into them in the supermarket, I always imagined Sam living in his office.

"Your dad told me a bit about what's been going on, Kitty, but I'd like to hear it from you."

I tell him about the comfortable lie: less a lie, I think, and more avoiding a harder truth.

"I just couldn't face a whole new city of people looking sad when they see me. I can't explain everything all over again, and I can't just say my mum's dead and expect someone to leave it at that. Nobody answers the statement 'My mum's dead' with 'Sorry about that, anyway, what did you think of the Spanish teacher?'"

"No, but you could say something like, 'My mum died a few months ago. It's tough for me to talk about, so I'd prefer not to.' How does that sound, Kitty?"

It sounds easy enough when he says it. I remember Imogen's words when I told her what had happened, "How do you get yourself into these situations, Kitty?" The answer is I don't know.

Sam says he thinks that it would be a good idea for me to talk to the therapist he recommended, so Dad calls Dr. Natasha Feld to make the appointment and is excited to hear she has a cancellation for Tuesday after school. I can't believe I have become the kind of girl who needs therapists on two continents. I google Dr.

Feld and learn from her website that she is "a licensed clinical psychologist providing compassionate individual psychotherapy services to children and adolescents experiencing symptoms of anxiety, depression, and challenges with life transitions and stressors." I also learn that she doesn't accept health insurance. Another Google search tells me that the average cost for an hour of therapy in NYC is a whopping two hundred fifty dollars! I hope she can fix me in one appointment. I google Sam, but he doesn't have a website. I wonder if we used to pay him at all. I can't imagine it.

When I arrive at Dr. Feld's office on Broadway, I can see why she has to charge so much. It's on the sixteenth floor of a swanky art deco building. Her office shares a floor with several other doctors and an expensive-looking spa called Zen. The hallway has a citrusy, minty smell, which I assume comes from there. I ride up in an old-fashioned elevator with a group of already beautiful women who don't look as if they need therapy or facials. None of them pays attention to the pale-faced girl watching them. They're too busy looking perfect and tapping on their phones. They waft out of the elevator as one.

I walk down the hallway, past the Zen spa, and open the door to room 1606. Inside is a cozy waiting room. In one corner of the room are six chairs and a large dark-wood coffee table with a pile of magazines and an orchid on it. In the other corner is a miniature version of the adult seating area, but the chairs are small, plastic, and all different colors. There is a low table with a range of children's books spread out on it and a tidy rack of papers and colored pens and pencils. More books are stacked on a shelf behind the chairs, along with an unusual assortment of stuffed animals. There's a flamingo with hot-pink plumage, an adorable baby raccoon, a family of skunks with pristine fur, an octopus, a narwhal, and a rainbow-colored herd of llamas. I'm tempted to go and have a closer look at the llamas but instead head to the grown-up area, which is where I suppose someone my age should sit. It's definitely where Imogen would sit.

A sign on the wall instructs you to push one of four buzzers. I carefully press the one with Dr. Feld's name next to it, but there's no sound, so I press it again. Nobody answers. I'll wait five minutes before trying one last time. Maybe she's not here and I can sneak home. On the wall is a framed picture of Dr. Feld from *New York* magazine's "Best Doctors in NYC" article. Ugh, I bet she costs way more than two hundred fifty dollars an hour. In the photo, she's wearing a floaty greenish-blue paisley dress and standing in front of a huge desk.

"Kitty?" says a low, soft voice from behind me. I turn and see Dr. Feld in the flesh. I think she might be wearing the same dress as in the picture. She has mahogany corkscrew curls twisted into a bun at the nape of her neck. At first, I think she has two chopsticks poking out of her bun, but I realize on closer inspection that they are pencils. I'm intrigued to see if she will pull one out to take notes during my appointment. There's a long streak of white running through one side of her hair, a bit like Cruella de Vil. Dr. Feld looks much kinder than Cruella de Vil, and I'm certain she would never wear fur. She looks like she might be vegan and probably has a rescue dog.

"Come this way," she says and leads me through into her office.

Inside the walls are a soft, pale green. It's an appropriately peaceful choice for a therapist's office. Still, I would have suggested a darker, richer green like color number 19, Lichen, "named after the ever-changing, subtle color of creeping algae," according to Farrow & Ball. There's a large box of tissues conveniently placed on the table. I suppose there are tissues in every therapist's office around the world. Sam had them too. Unlike in Sam's office, where the only greenery is an ailing spider plant, Dr. Feld has an impressive collection of small moss-filled terrariums that smell like damp grass cuttings, in the best way. I must email Sam to tell him about the terrariums and consider asking Dr. Feld if I can take a picture of them on my phone to send to him later.

"Make yourself comfortable," she says, waving an arm in the direction of the sofa. She sits down gracefully in one of the chairs while I sink clumsily into the couch. It feels as if it's going to be a struggle to get out of it.

"It's nice to meet you, Kitty. Why don't you start by telling me a little bit about yourself and what brings you here today? As I always say—kids need to know how much I care before they care to know how much I know!"

Wow, did she really just say that? I make a mental note to tell Sam this gem. Dr. Feld opens a large green notepad and, to my great disappointment, produces a pen from between its pages, leaving the pencils in her bun untouched. I'm impressed to see that the notebook cover matches the walls. Maybe Dr. Feld is a color person too. Mindful of the cost, I get straight to the point.

"My mum died in March, we just moved to New York for three months, nobody here knows my mum's dead, and I kind of let people think she's still alive. I'm here to find out what I should do to sort it all out."

Dr. Feld scribbles a few notes and nods vigorously, causing the enormous silver hoop earrings she's wearing to bob up and down. I notice one of the dark corkscrew curls has escaped from her bun and wound its way around the hoop.

"Tell me more, Kitty," she says, and I try my best to stop staring at the curl trapped in her left earring. She might think I have a lazy eye, plus I really ought to concentrate, given how much this must be costing Dad.

"So, I'm here today because my dad says I'm not dealing with things well, and my sister, Imogen, thinks I'm a weirdo."

"And what do you think?"

"Sam, the therapist I saw in London, used to say that going through grief was like Snakes and Ladders. This might have been a snake."

Dr. Feld looks confused.

"You know, the board game. Down the snakes and up the ladders?" I add helpfully.

"Oh, you mean Chutes and Ladders?"

"Oh, yes." I remember Sam telling me that. "Well, we call it Snakes and Ladders in England."

"And we call it Chutes and Ladders here. I think that's an excellent description of the grieving process. Sam sounds like a smart guy!"

He is, and much cheaper. Possibly free. I'm starting to find Dr. Natasha Feld quite annoying.

"One of my sayings, Kitty, is that grief is a multitasking emotion. Does that resonate with you?" Dr. Feld asks.

I have no idea what she means, but I try to look as if I understand. Dr. Feld is clearly not buying my look of competence since she goes on.

"Let me put it a different way—grief can trigger all kinds of emotions, and people cycle through them in different ways and at different speeds. Have you heard of the seven stages of grief?"

Obviously, I know that—it's Grief 101. I suddenly picture the 101 Dalmatians looking sad, tiny tears rolling down their sweet little black-and-white-spotted faces. It must be Dr. Feld's Cruella de Vil hair that makes me think of the Dalmatian puppies.

Dr. Feld continues. "Well, like your Sam, I don't believe grief is a linear process. Grief doesn't move in one direction, from denial to pain to anger, and so on. People who are grieving bounce back and forth between the stages, sometimes in the same minute. I also believe there is another stage of grief. Can you guess what that is?"

It strikes me that Dr. Feld talks a lot more than Sam ever did. I shake my head.

"Joy!" she says triumphantly, hoop earrings swinging wildly, releasing the trapped curl. I almost cheer. "Yes, Kitty. You look surprised. Many people do when I tell them. It's actually a core theme of the book I've written: *Heal Your Pain with Joy.*"

I think that's a terrible title for her book. It sounds as if Dr. Feld's first name is Joy, but I know from her website it's Natasha. Dr. Feld's face takes on a softer, serious expression.

"I'm sure your mother brought you so much joy, and I'm equally sure you brought her tremendous happiness. Now, I wonder if in letting Ava and her mom think your mom is still alive, you were indulging in escapism. Denial of your reality, if you will. Enabling some joy."

"Maybe?" I say doubtfully.

Dr. Feld beams at me as if I have just cracked a difficult code.

"Excellent, Kitty, really excellent work. Well, we're out of time for today, but let's explore more of this topic next week. Until then, here's a copy of my book. I signed it for you. There are some exercises at the back. Why don't you try doing the first one before our next appointment?" Dr. Feld hands me a thick hard-backed copy of *Heal Your Pain with Joy*, a serene-looking, black-and-white photo of her on the front cover, and the subtitle in curly letters—*The Only Cure for Grief is to Grieve*.

"Um, thanks," I say as she gently herds me to the door.

Only good manners stop me from dropping the book into the recycling bin on my way out of the office. In the hallway, I see a familiar figure loping toward the elevator—Henry. Could he have been at the Zen spa? Quite possibly. He does have great skin. I scan the hall for a convenient pillar to hide behind, but nothing. There's no way to avoid him, and he's not going to think

I've been to the spa unless it's for mustache waxing. Not that I have a mustache, but he might think I do.

"Hi, Henry," I say, trying to sound casual.

"Oh, hi, Kitty." Henry smiles as if it's quite natural to run into me in this random building on Broadway. I'm not going to ask him what he's doing here. He might be embarrassed to be seen leaving the spa.

"I just saw my therapist," he says as if this were nothing. "Tuesdays and Thursdays, after school, ever since my mom and dad separated."

"Me too. It was my first therapy session here. I'm just doing Tuesdays. My mum died in March."

Oddly, it seems simple to tell Henry the truth that I couldn't tell Ava. He's easier to talk to than the other kids at school. I sometimes feel like Ava and the rest of the girls are waiting for me to say or do something dumb.

"God, I'm so sorry, Kitty. That sucks."

He reaches out a hand as if he's going to pat me on the shoulder, but then thinks better of it and drops his arm back to his side.

We get into the elevator together, and I continue. I'm babbling now.

"And then I sort of let Ava and her mum think that my mum's still alive. Ava's mum wanted my mum to be on the Halloween dance committee and kept asking me for her number. Then she asked my dad, and that's how he found out I'd pretended Mum is still alive and how I ended up here. I'm going to have to tell Ava the truth. She'll think I'm a complete freak."

Henry studies me intently. He doesn't look at me as if I'm a freak.

"I doubt it," he says. "Ava's surprisingly chill. She was great when my dad and his girlfriend were all over Page Six."

I must look confused, and while we walk out of the building, Henry waving goodbye to the doorman, he explains that Page Six is a gossip column in the *New York Post*.

"They run these blind items: 'Which married, green-eyed actor was caught looking very friendly with his delicious young French leading lady in a Williamsburg bar this week?' That was the end of my mom and dad being married."

He sighs and is looking at his shoes when a vintage sports car pulls up to the curb.

"Hey, Henry," the driver yells. "Come on, get in."

I recognize Henry's dad from the Google search I'd done after Ava told me about him. I have to admit he is good-looking, even though he's old. With his dark hair, too long for most dads to pull off, emerald-green eyes, and chiseled cheekbones, James Davenport radiates glamor. He looks like someone in a commercial for an expensive Swiss watch. Now I come to think about it; maybe he has been in one of those ads. I'm sure I have a memory of his brooding face staring at me from the pages of a magazine. People on the sidewalk around us are looking at him and starting to pull out their phones, and an excited buzz begins. James Davenport responds by revving the engine and scowling at them, which only makes him look more film-star-like.

"I'd better go," Henry says, wincing at the noise of the car. "Can we give you a ride home, Kitty?"

"God, no!" I say. "I mean, no thanks."

"Okay. See you tomorrow then. I'm so sorry about your mom."

The idea of me riding through the streets of SoHo with Henry and his film-star dad in an open-top car makes me giggle—it's so surreal. I watch as Henry and his dad pull out into the busy street. I hear whispers around me: "That was definitely James Davenport," "OMG, I wish I'd taken a selfie with him," "Do you think that was his kid with the blue hair? He didn't look much like him, did he? He looked kind of weird." I feel like shouting at the gathered crowd, "Yes, that is his kid, and guess what— he's not at all weird. In fact, he's a lot nicer and more interesting than his dad will ever be."

I continue walking to the subway station and try to

imagine what it would be like to have a famous dad—
one who picks you up from therapy appointments in a
midnight-blue sports car. It's impossible to imagine my
dad driving a sports car, let alone cheating on Mum. The
only newspaper article about them would have been a
picture of him kissing my mum's bald head underneath
the headline "True Love."

"How was your appointment with Dr. Feld?" asks Dad
when I walk into the apartment. I think he must have
warned Imogen not to comment since she is sitting quietly at the table, pretending to do her homework.

"It was okay, I guess. She has a streak of white in her
hair, like Cruella de Vil."

Dad looks confused.

"You know, Cruella de Vil, the baddie in *101 Dalmatians*. By the way, how much does Dr. Feld charge?"

"Never mind that, Kitty. Did you find it helpful to
talk to her?"

I suppose I did, although I think I found it more useful
to talk to Henry afterward. I hesitate before speaking.

"I saw that boy from school, Henry Davenport, at the
therapist's office. He was seeing a different therapist."

"Oooooh, is he the one with the famous dad?" Imogen
says. "How cool is that?"

"He picked Henry up from the appointment."

"Nice! Did you get a lift home with them? You can be therapy buddies." My sister probably thinks she'll get an invitation to the Oscars if Henry and I become friends.

"No, Henry offered, but I said I was taking the subway."

"Why, Kitty, why? Why would any normal person take the stinky old subway instead of getting a ride home with a movie star and his presumably gorgeous son? No wonder you need to see a therapist."

Imogen's brief dalliance with sympathy and tact has clearly screeched to a grinding halt.

"That's enough, Imogen," says Dad, the warning in his voice unmistakable. "I don't think you're old enough to be riding around New York with boys, Kitty."

"I'm not riding around anywhere. Didn't you hear me say I took the subway?"

"Quite right, too. Even Imogen might be a bit young to have a boyfriend, but I suppose Josh is harmless enough."

Imogen looks annoyed to hear her boyfriend described as harmless. I'm not sure if their long-distance relationship is working out well. They don't seem to have been FaceTiming nearly as much as they used to when we first moved. Trouble in paradise?

"Does Henry have an older brother?" Imogen asks,

tilting her head to one side.

"No. Lucky him, he's an only child," I reply.

Ava doesn't seem at all surprised when I tell her about Mum the next day after school, so I suppose her mum already talked to her. Even thinking about that conversation makes my face feel hot.

"That's so sad. I can't even imagine what it must be like for you. I mean, my grandpa died, but that's not the same, is it? We were really, really close, though. His funeral was so sad. There must have been like two hundred people there. My mom said half the golf club showed up to pay their respects. I cried for days. I did a reading at the funeral. Did you do a reading for your mom? Anyway, when I did the reading, everyone else started crying and said it was the most moving thing ever."

As I walk down the subway stairs to my platform, I see Ava's train is already there. She waves at me through the window and makes a heart with her thumbs and index fingers. I give her a half wave back as her train leaves the station. So now Mum's dead in New York as well. Even though I know it was wrong, there was something lovely about having people think she might turn up at school or help organize the Halloween dance. I know Imogen would say I'm weird and it probably proves that I do need therapy, but it made me happy, just for a minute, to have her back. Perhaps I did steal a few moments of joy.

When I get home from school, I pick up the copy of Dr. Feld's book, *Heal Your Pain with Joy*, and flip to the exercises at the end. The first one is to write a letter to the person who died. There are different templates for the letter. I pick the one called "Three Things," grab a pen and paper, and begin to write.

Dear Mum,

I miss you every single day. When I can't get to sleep at night, which happens a lot, I think of three happy memories of you—I'm not even close to running out of them. Memories that make me feel safe and cozy. Here are the three I thought of last night.

The time I was home from school with chicken pox, and you painted little dots of red all over your face, and then we laughed until we cried at the look on Dad's face when he got home.

That morning in the garden at Kate's house when we made a daisy chain so long it could go around both our shoulders and still reach the ground. We wore it like that all through lunch, entwined in the white petals with their sunny little faces and green arms and legs.

The time when you let me do your hair and makeup before we went out for pizza, and even though Imogen said it looked awful and it did, you left it on and grinned at me all evening across the table through the blue eye shadow and bright-pink lipstick. You looked so beautiful.

I love you so much. I miss you so much.

Kitty xxx

I wipe my tears, fold the paper as many times as I can until it is a tiny square, and tuck it at the very back of my desk drawer. Exercise one is complete.

CHAPTER EIGHTEEN

GLUTEN-FREE GRANOLA

"Come on, girls. We're going to be late for brunch."

"Why do we have to go all the way to the West Village for brunch?" asks Imogen.

"It's nice to try new places," says Dad.

I don't like trying new places, particularly when the best pancakes I've ever tasted are five blocks from this sofa. The restaurant we're going to is called Founding Farmers. I usually love a business with a pun for a name—"The Mane Event" hair salon, "Freudian Sip" coffee shop, and "A Walk in the Bark" pet store are some of my personal favorites—but I don't see why we need to walk for forty minutes to get brunch.

"The friends we're having brunch with said this place has the most amazing pancakes, Kitty." Dad smiles at me.

"What friends?" I say. "Someone from work?"

"A friend of mine named Jen. She's bringing her son, Dashiell. Everyone calls him Dash."

"Dash?" I say. "What kind of name is Dash? He sounds like a reindeer."

"Says the girl named what a toddler calls a cat!" says Imogen. "But seriously, Dad, who even are these people?"

"Just friends," says Dad. "Come on. We're late. We're going to have to get a cab now."

As soon as Dad takes off his coat and hands it to the server, I notice he's wearing new jeans and a new sweater, both unusually tight-fitting.

"Are they skinny jeans?" I ask him.

Imogen leans down to inspect his legs.

"Dad, we talked about this. No skinny jeans over forty. Also, you need a straight-leg jean with your thighs. That is not a good look for you. Not a good look at all."

I almost feel sorry for Dad until I notice a tall woman standing a few tables away from us. She has shoulder-length caramel-colored, wavy hair and holds her hand up in greeting. Dad waves back and starts weaving his way between the tables to reach her and a little boy who is sitting on a booster seat, smashing a toy car repeatedly into the salt and pepper shakers.

"Imogen, Kitty, meet Jen and Dashiell." Dad stands there looking awkward, and nobody speaks for about a minute.

"Hi, girls," says Jen, dazzling us with her impossibly straight white teeth. I can't help but compare them to Dad's. His teeth are a bit crooked and resemble a before photo, which could adorn the wall at Jen's orthodontist. He's also grinning in a frankly idiotic way. "It's so great to finally meet you. I've heard so much about you both!"

When did she hear so much about us both? Imogen and I exchange loaded glances as we take our seats on either side of Dad, unconsciously boxing him in.

"Dash, can you say hi to Imogen and Kitty?"

"Where's the kitty?" he says in a high lispy voice. Imogen snorts.

"I'm the kitty," I tell him. "I mean, I'm Kitty. It's my name."

Dash looks at me skeptically, apparently too young to have registered that he's named after Santa's second favorite reindeer. He studies me for a moment longer before going back to destroying the salt and pepper shakers.

"So," says Imogen, leaning forward in the manner of an investigative journalist. "You guys work together?"

Jen and Dad exchange glances.

"Actually, no. We met through friends," Dad says.

"Who?" I ask.

"Nobody that you know," he says in a weirdly high-pitched voice, not looking at me. "Now, let's order. I'm starving."

"Your dad says you love pancakes, Kitty. You have to try them here. They're yummy, right Dash?" says Jen.

"I want pancakes," he says.

"No thanks," I say, "just coffee for me. I'm not hungry."

Dad raises an eyebrow but doesn't comment on the fact that a) I have never drunk coffee in my life, and b) I always dramatically gag at the smell when he makes it at home.

"Well, I'm starving," Imogen says. "French toast for me please."

So much for sisterly solidarity. Obviously, I'm hungry too, but I'm protesting about having to have brunch with this mysterious woman and her annoying child. I glare at my sister for not joining me in my mini hunger strike, but she is totally oblivious and has started chatting with the kid. She's probably hoping his mum will ask her to babysit. She told me a girl in her grade gets twenty dollars an hour for looking after a neighbor's kid.

Dad orders a spinach-and-feta egg-white omelet, and

Jen has gluten-free granola and an iced almond-milk matcha latte. I have no idea what that is, but it sounds ridiculously pretentious.

"Why aren't you having eggs Benedict, Dad?" I ask loudly. "You always have eggs Benedict."

"I'm trying to cut down on nitrates."

"What's a nitrate?" asks Dash.

"It's something super unhealthy they put in bacon and ham to make them last longer," says Jen.

"I don't like nitrates," Dash announces to the table at large.

I roll my eyes at him. The waiter pours me a muddy-looking cup of coffee and asks again if I'm sure I don't want to order anything to eat. He clearly thinks Dad is a terrible parent allowing his kid to drink coffee. I try not to gag at the smell.

Dash's stack of pancakes has arrived, and he's drowning them in maple syrup. Clearly, Jen has been reading so much about nitrates she's missed the articles on the dangers of sugar. The smell of bacon coming from the kitchen is making my mouth water. I should have ordered a plate of bacon, a whole dish of nitrates.

"So, Kitty, how do you like school? Dash goes there too. He's in junior kindergarten."

Well, I suppose that solves the question of which of

Dad's "friends" recommended the school.

For the next forty-five painful minutes, I pretend to drink my coffee and try not to stare longingly at Imogen's French toast, which she's drenched with syrup, berries, and whipped cream. I guess the Glow-Up Challenge must be over. She probably won. My stomach rumbles angrily, and Dash giggles and points at me. I sit there sulking and wishing I'd ordered something to eat while everyone else chats cheerfully. Eventually, Dash drops his trucks on the floor and has a complete meltdown.

"Sorry," says Jen, picking him up. "He gets tired and cranky right about now." Dash rests his curly head on her shoulder and sticks his thumb in his mouth.

"I know the feeling," I mutter as everyone bustles around, gathering their things, and we head out of the restaurant.

The early October breeze is whipping up hundreds of little white peaks on the surface of the Hudson River as we walk home. I look across the water and try and fail to remember the name of New Jersey's capital. Imogen's droning on about a party she wants to go to on Friday evening and why her curfew should be midnight. Well, if she's not going to ask, then I will.

"Who was that?"

"It was a friend of Dad's named Jen and her son, Dashiell," Imogen says. "You're not the sharpest tool in the box, are you, Kitty?"

"Don't be mean, Imogen," Dad says. "Actually, it's pretty interesting how we met. We met online, on a parenting forum."

"Flying Solo?" I ask, without stopping to think.

"How on earth do you know about Flying Solo?" says Dad, turning to look at me in astonishment.

"I'm a member. Ages ago, I was checking your computer for dating websites. It was after that night you and Dominic talked about you getting married again." Dad's face has gone from surprised to annoyed in the space of ten seconds, but I continue. "Anyway, I didn't find any sketchy websites, well, I didn't think I had. I thought Flying Solo was for bereaved parents, not a . . . a hookup site."

Imogen lets out a snort of laughter at me calling it a hookup site, and Dad lets out a deep sigh and gazes out across the river. I suspect he's counting to ten in his head.

"Kitty, how many times do you have to be told not to snoop? If you must know, yes, we did meet on Flying Solo. I was looking for advice about New York, and Jen was extremely helpful with suggestions."

I bet she was.

"What was she doing on there, anyway?" I ask.

"Jen's husband died in a car accident before Dash was even born. As you should know, given you've visited Flying Solo, it's a forum for parents who've lost their partners and are doing their very best to raise their children alone."

"So she's not your girlfriend?" I ask, relieved.

"No, Jen is not my girlfriend!"

Thank goodness for that. We walk on in silence.

That evening I go to Flying Solo to delete my account. I'm pretty sure Dad won't ever post here again now that he knows I come on the site, so there's no point in having an account. I scroll back through his old posts. The last ones were posted from London, when he was looking for advice about the move to New York. My eye falls on one of the responses to an earlier question of his. I remember noticing it the first time I logged into the site. "D's dad died before he was born and I'm sure I talk about him way too much. D seems to love hearing stories about his dad, but he's only four. I'll see how it goes as he gets older. Good luck. JDNYC." JDNYC must be short for Jen and Dash New York City. It feels bizarre to be able to put a face, actually two faces, to her post. I think about searching on her username and reading more of her posts, but that seems wrong, like a grubby thing to do. I go to the admin page to shut down my account, the cursor hovering over the Delete Account button. I don't check the box but close the window instead. I'm not ready to be flying solo.

CHAPTER NINETEEN

TRICK OR TREAT

Halloween is huge in New York. Everyone seems to go trick-or-treating, and even pets wear costumes. Ava's dog, Diva, is dressing as the pope. When I tell Gran about this, she says it is sacrilegious for anyone but the pope to wear a papal costume, let alone a dachshund.

"Diva looks adorable in it. She even has a little miter headpiece," I say to Gran, but I can tell, even though we're not on FaceTime, that she's frowning.

Pets aren't allowed at the Halloween dance. Principal Carter had sent parents an email containing the rules for the evening. Unfortunately, the families of students are invited to the dance and encouraged to join in the fun with their own costumes.

Imogen is going trick-or-treating with her friends

dressed as an improbably attractive zombie bride. I had suggested she go as a superhero with an extending ponytail armed with scrunchies, but she looked at me like I was crazy. Her nod to her living-dead status seems to be a darker-than-usual smoky eye, pale-blue lipstick, and a shredded veil.

"Shouldn't you have pieces of flesh falling off and things?" I ask as I watch her perfect her dewy skin. "I'm pretty sure that zombies don't wear highlighter."

The decorating committee has been working around the clock. Parent volunteers have transformed the hallways and gym with dozens of fuzzy paper bats, cutouts of black cats with arched backs, spooky skeletons, cauldrons, and jack-o'-lanterns. I saw Jen from a distance one day but didn't go to say hello. She was pinning up witches' hats and broomsticks. Someone has hung long, white chiffon ghosts from the branches of the trees around the playground. The ghosts sway elegantly in the October breeze. The whole scene looks less like a school dance and more like a spread in *Vogue*, which makes sense given that Ava's mum is in charge of the decorating committee, and she used to be a magazine editor.

"Is it always this big a deal?" I ask Henry before class starts.

"Yup. Halloween, the Winterfest, and School Spirit Week are all totally over the top. Winterfest is the worst because glitter gets everywhere."

I consider telling Henry about the grief glitter that Gran had talked about as we walked down the hill in London all those months ago. The image has stuck in my mind. I still find grief glitter all the time. I thought I might have left enormous silver piles of it behind in London, but I still discover specks of it every day. Instead, I ask him about his costume.

"Same as last year," he says.

"I wasn't here last Halloween," I remind him.

"Oh, that's right. Well, I'm always a vampire because it's easy—black cloak, fangs, and some fake blood. I keep forgetting you've only been here for a few months. It feels like you've been here forever. In a good way, I mean."

I raise an eyebrow, and he blushes a little.

"How about you?" Henry asks.

"A rabbit," I say, embarrassed, but there's no time to explain as Ms. Lyons walks into the room. It's Henry's turn to raise an eyebrow, and I blush, a lot.

Ava has used her significant powers of persuasion to convince a group of girls in the seventh grade to dress as characters from *Alice in Wonderland*. Ava has the most amazing Queen of Hearts costume, and the rest of us are just along for the ride. Maddie, who has long blond hair, is Alice, and Lulu is the Mad Hatter. Ava said I could choose between the White Rabbit or the Cheshire Cat. I chose the rabbit, because it seemed like an easier costume. I'm wearing bunny ears, one of which keeps drooping over my eye, a blue jacket of Dad's, a white scarf, and have attempted to draw whiskers on my face with Imogen's favorite eyeliner. I also have a gold-colored pocket watch bought for $6.99 from a costume shop that sprang up on Broadway near Dr. Feld's office. It is the most effort I've ever put into a costume, but Ava is taking the whole thing incredibly seriously. I just hope it will be good enough.

That evening the playground is packed with little unicorns, Pokémon, cats, and witches, all charging around hopped up on sugar. I see four kids dressed as sushi rolls and two as tacos.

The teachers are kept busy confiscating lightsabers, swords, plastic caveman clubs, and other weapons. Apparently, their parents didn't read that part of the memo, and a few Luke Skywalkers are having complete meltdowns, which is hardly appropriate behavior for a Jedi Knight. When we get to the gym, we find Dash, dressed as Yoda, sobbing as the junior kindergarten teacher takes away his green lightsaber.

"You can have it back at the end of the dance, Dashiell," the teacher says kindly.

Jen looks ridiculous dressed as Princess Leia with a brown wig complete with plaited buns on each ear. Dad is dressed as a pirate and gets his cutlass confiscated, much to Jen's amusement.

"Don't worry, Rob. You can have it back at the end of the dance," Jen tells him.

I roll my eyes and move on, still suspicious of Dad having an attractive female friend. I feel self-conscious dressed as a white rabbit out of context, and when an eighth-grade boy asks me if I'm supposed to be dressed as a Playboy bunny, I go to look for the rest of Wonderland. I find the girls huddled together gossiping about Henry's dad, who has just strolled in with his latest model girlfriend in tow. He's dressed as the Big Bad Wolf, and his girlfriend is a less-than-wholesome-looking Little Red Riding Hood.

"He's wearing that wolf mask so he doesn't get photographed," says Ava knowingly.

"Well, his girlfriend is dressed as if she wants to!" says Lulu.

She's not wrong. James Davenport's girlfriend is wearing white over-the-knee socks, a minuscule red gingham dress that looks like she might have repurposed it from an Oktoberfest costume, and the ubiquitous little red hood. Principal Carter, who is dressed as a Minion, is looking nervous and sweaty. Perhaps he's worried he's going to get complaints from parents about sexy Red Riding Hood.

Ava and the rest of Wonderland are in the middle of the dance floor, swirling around and singing the lyrics of a song I've only ever heard coming from under the door of Imogen's room. I feel self-conscious enough in my costume, and there's no way I'm going to start leaping around in front of everyone. I'm a fish out of water, or a rabbit out of its warren. I wonder how long we'll have to stay. Dad is happily chatting with Principal Carter and Ava's mum, who is wearing a brilliant Maleficent costume, which looks as if it came straight from the movie. It probably did. I head over to tell Dad I'm going to the loo and wander off, away from the noise of music, laughter, and a few tears—probably the mini–Luke Skywalkers still mourning the loss of the best part of their costumes. There's a long line for the bathrooms nearest the gym, so I go upstairs, even though it's off-limits during the dance.

The second-floor hallway is dimly lit, deserted, and blissfully quiet. The idea of going back downstairs is overwhelming. It won't do any harm to disappear for half an hour or so. Then I can go back to the gym, find Dad, and it will be time to go home. I slip silently into the library. It's a bit dark and spooky in there, but I can see well enough to find a book and take it to the bathroom to read. A rustling sound ahead stops me in my tracks; someone or something is in here! The rustling noise happens again, definitely too big to be a rat. Maybe it's another socially awkward individual trying to escape the mayhem of the gym. Either way, I don't want to see them, so I begin to tiptoe back to the door. Suddenly a light appears in the direction of the noise. It's Henry, lying on the beanbags usually occupied by the kindergarteners during story time and pointing the flashlight on his phone right at me.

"Kitty! What are you doing here? I thought I was going to get busted by one of the teachers."

"You're not supposed to be in here," I say unnecessarily. God, why did I say that? It makes it sound as though I'm on duty patrolling the school, looking for infractions. I sit down clumsily on a beanbag. Even Imogen wouldn't be able to sit on one of these things gracefully.

"I know. Neither are you."

"Are you hiding from your dad? I saw him downstairs. He's the wolf, right?"

Please let me stop saying such stupid things. I say a

silent prayer to the god of tween girls who are talking to boys they may or may not like to make me more eloquent, or better still, sound vaguely cool.

"That's him," Henry says with bitterness in his voice. "I don't know why he bothered coming. When I was younger, and I wanted him here, he never showed up, too busy working or whatever he was doing. That costume my dad's girlfriend is wearing sums up the difference between my mom and every girlfriend my dad has ever had."

"What do you mean?"

"I mean if my parents were still married, mom would have dressed as a cool grandmother, not an X-rated Little Red Riding Hood."

"My dad came as a pirate. One of the teachers confiscated his cutlass."

Henry laughs. He still has some fake blood on his chin, but he's taken out the vampire fangs.

"I like your ears, Kitty," he says, reaching over to move the one that's flopping into my eye.

"Thanks," I say, blushing and jumping up. I trip over the corner of the beanbag in my rush to get to the door.

"Kitty," says Henry. He's leaning up on one elbow and looking totally and impossibly cute. "Thanks for cheering me up."

"You're welcome." I race out of the library. As I stumble down the stairs, I can't suppress my grin. Maybe this costume wasn't such a terrible idea after all. Perhaps I should even thank Ava.

CHAPTER TWENTY

COLOR THERAPY

My jaw nearly hits my desk on Monday morning when a brown-haired Henry walks into the classroom. His hair isn't quite Mouse's Back. More of a London Stone, color number six, which I remember the website described as "effortlessly modern and utterly timeless." This description stuck with me, as London Stone is the color I tried to convince myself my hair was for a long time.

"What happened to your hair?" asks Ava, staring at Henry. "I haven't seen it this color since like fifth grade!"

"I felt like a change. Is that okay with you?" Henry says in an uncharacteristically surly voice. He slumps into the desk behind Ava and me. Ava rolls her eyes and mouths "touchy." I wish Henry sat in front of me so I could examine his hair color. I risk turning around a couple of times to take a look. Both times he has his arms folded on his desk making a pillow for his London Stone head. He's not even doodling.

Today is my sixth meeting with Dr. Feld. While I've grown used to her huge hoop earrings and floaty dresses, I miss Sam with his creased denim shirts and equally creased face. Dr. Feld is remarkably wrinkle-free; maybe she gets a discount at the Zen spa.

"So, Kitty, how has everything been this week?" Dr. Feld asks in her husky voice. She always sounds as if she's recovering from a sore throat.

"Fine."

"Did you have a fun Halloween?"

"It was okay." Wow, this is really not worth two hundred and fifty dollars per hour.

"What did you do?"

"My school had a dance."

"Ah, yes, the dance that your friend"—she pauses to consult her notes—"Ava's mom wanted your mom to help with."

Wow, she's good. Way to turn the Halloween dance back to the reason I came to therapy in the first place.

"And how has it been since then? You told me that you'd talked to Ava. Do you talk to anyone else about your mom? Apart from your dad and your sister?"

"My gran, my godmother, my friend Jessica, and Sam when I talk to him." I don't mention Henry.

"So nobody in New York?"

"No. Why would I? It's not like I live here or anything."

"But you do live here, Kitty. Even though you aren't here for long, I do believe it's important for you to integrate your mom into your new life. However temporary your time in New York is, your experience of it is part of your narrative."

My narrative? What's she talking about?

"My narrative?"

"Yes, Kitty, your narrative. Now, let's do an exercise about the future. This one is from my new book—*Life After Loss: Love Is the Answer.*" Dr. Feld hands me a large piece of paper and a pen. "Most people think that therapy is about the past, but it's actually all about the future. What do you want your next chapter to be, Kitty?"

She really does come up with the worst titles for her books. I sit, pen in hand, staring stupidly at the blank sheet of paper on the coffee table in front of me. Dr. Feld looks at me expectantly, so I write Kitty Wentworth and the date and then underline the words twice. She nods encouragingly, bouncing her earrings around, as if now that I've put pen to paper, the words will magically flood out. They don't. I watch as she stops nodding and her hoop earrings become still.

"I don't know what to write," I say eventually. "What on earth am I supposed to write?"

"It's your story, Kitty. Only you can know."

"Well, I don't know, okay?"

"Interesting, why do you think that might be?"

Dr. Feld's dumb question makes me want to throw the pen at her.

"Kitty?"

"I don't want my story. I hate it. I want the story I had before. This isn't what my life is supposed to be. I want to rip out all the pages from the last year and go back to having my mum."

I'm crying now. Not gentle, therapeutic cleansing tears but great big sloppy, snotty gulping sobs. Dr. Feld pushes the tissues toward me, but I ignore them and continue through the mucus.

"I need a story where my mum gets better, where we stay in London, where I'm not sitting in this office having to talk to you with this stupid piece of paper in front of me."

Dr. Feld sits quietly for a long time until I've stopped sobbing and blown my nose with a loud honking noise.

It takes about seven tissues to clear the snot. That crying fit probably cost my dad a hundred dollars, but to my surprise, I do feel better, lighter, as if a stone in my throat that was preventing me from swallowing has dislodged. I haven't cried like this in a really long time.

"I still haven't written anything," I say eventually, holding up the paper. Several tears have splashed onto my name, causing the black ink of the letters to merge.

"I think you've achieved a lot today, Kitty. Without writing a word you put some important chapter headings for your future: headings like Love, Resilience, and Courage. Let's leave it there for this week."

Dr. Feld closes her notebook with a snap and guides me to the door.

"Very well done, Kitty. Remember, grief is a multitasking emotion."

When I walk out of Dr. Feld's office, Henry is leaning against the wall next to the elevator, his brown hair covered in a baseball cap.

"Hi," I say, sniffing and stuffing the handful of soggy tissues and blank piece of paper into my coat pocket. If Henry notices my red, puffy eyes, he doesn't mention them.

"Want to walk to the subway together?"

"Sure," I say, but I'm not sure. I hope nobody from

school sees us. They might think we're on a date. Ava says quite a few kids in my grade are dating, and she knows everything that is going on in seventh grade. I blush at the thought of her seeing Henry and me together. We climb into the old elevator, which for once is empty. Henry sighs as he jabs the button for the lobby.

"I did it to piss my dad off. My hair, I mean. We had a big argument after the Halloween dance about him and his girlfriend turning up in their stupid costumes. When your hair's been six colors in the last two years, going back to brown seemed the best way to wind him up. It worked; he hates it. Dad says it makes me look like the son of an accountant. I wish my dad was an accountant instead of a dumb movie star. My therapist says me changing my hair is a healthy expression of rage. It does seem like a pretty lame way to rebel. I need to think of something more dramatic." Henry turns to look at me, a wry smile on his face. "What do you think?"

"I think the color protest is very eloquent, and it won't fry your brain, well, unless you're using some kind of toxic hair coloring. I like your natural hair color, by the way. It's London Stone. You're lucky. My hair is Mouse's Back."

"What are you talking about, Kitty?" Henry asks, looking baffled by my mention of rodents.

"My hair color is Mouse's Back." Henry still looks

confused, so I decide to explain as best I can. "I'm really into these paints by an English company called Farrow & Ball. They make the most gorgeous colors and give them the best names. They're called things like Arsenic, Elephant's Breath, and Dead Salmon."

"Geez, Dead Salmon!" Who would paint a room with that?"

"Lots of people. My godmother, Kate, is an interior designer, and she uses it all the time, especially in dining rooms. By candlelight, it's very flattering. She tells her older clients it will take twenty years off them, and that her services are much cheaper than a face lift."

"She sounds funny."

"She is. She was my mum's best friend."

The elevator arrives in the lobby, and a group of serene-looking spa-goers/therapy patients stands aside while we exit. As we walk into the chilly November evening, we fall into a companionable silence.

"Henry," I say after half a block, "does your therapist say weird things?"

"God, all the time," he groans. "He mostly talks like Yoda. 'If no mistakes you have made, but losing you are, a different game you should play.'"

I snort with laughter.

"He did not say that!"

"Something like that. I don't listen half the time."

"Dr. Feld says I need to create my own narrative."

"You need to do what now?"

"Exactly. She says I need to write it with resilience and bravery and that grief is a multitasking emotion."

"Where do they get this stuff from?" Henry says, shaking his head. "Anyway, I think you're brave."

"I'm not. I had an awful thing happen to me, that's all."

"Exactly, something really terrible happened, and here you are, on the other side of the world, getting on with your life. I'm just here because my dad can't stop dating girls half his age, and my mom can't stop drinking." Henry pauses, embarrassed. "I didn't mean to say that about my mom. It's been tough for her. Mom's great, though. Not so great when she's been drinking, but mostly great."

"It's okay. I won't tell anyone," I say.

We get to the subway station, and suddenly I don't care if anyone sees us together anymore. I give Henry an awkward smile.

"I think you're brave, too. If you ever want to talk about parent stuff, I'm happy to listen," I tell him.

"I feel bad complaining about my pathetic problems after what happened with your mom," Henry says, shuffling his feet.

"Don't feel bad. I want to talk about normal stuff—like people's parents being annoying."

"There's nothing normal about my family," Henry laughs. "Thanks, Kitty. You're a cool girl."

"Thanks," I say and give him a half wave as we go down different staircases to our platforms. Imogen would fall over in amazement if she knew a film star's son thinks I'm a cool girl. Imogen would fall over in amazement if she knew anyone at all thinks I'm a cool girl.

CHAPTER TWENTY-ONE

TURKEY DAY

Gran, who has been planning her visit to spend Thanksgiving in New York since we left London, unexpectedly announces a week before she is due to arrive that Mrs. Allison will be accompanying her.

"I didn't realize they are friends now," Dad says.

"Well, they do go to Pilates together once a week and are in a club called Aging with Attitude—whatever that is," I tell him.

"I dread to think."

When the duo walks into the arrivals area at JFK, they look like the most unlikely traveling companions. Mrs. Allison is sporting athleisure wear and wheeling a gigantic giraffe-print suitcase trimmed with fuchsia. No chance of picking up the wrong bag from the carousel with that luggage. Gran has a sensible small navy-blue bag.

"Is Mrs. Allison wearing leggings?" asks Dad weakly.

"She appears to be, but don't worry, Gran is in her usual wrinkle-free travel trousers," I tell him.

"Thank goodness for that."

Dad orders an Uber for the journey into Manhattan, and while we wait for it to arrive, Mrs. Allison tells us the plot lines of the two movies she watched on the flight.

"Did you watch a film, Gran?" I ask.

"Absolutely not," she says. "I stood for much of the flight. You read about people my age suffering from deep vein thrombosis, but there's no blood pooling here." Gran lifts one leg of her sensible traveling trousers and flicks the top of a tight-fitting skin-colored sock, which comes up to her knee. "That and drinking plenty of water are key to healthy air travel."

"Sexy socks, Gran!" says Imogen. "Are you hoping for a holiday romance?"

Gran ignores her.

"Well, I wiggled my toes while I watched the films," says Mrs. Allison. "And I had plenty to drink during the flight."

"White wine doesn't count, Elizabeth. Alcoholic drinks actually have a dehydrating effect on the system," Gran says.

"I don't see how. I needed to go to the toilet every half hour, so it must have been going through my system!"

★ ★ ★

Our apartment is too small for Gran and Mrs. Allison to stay with us, so Dad has booked them into a hotel a few blocks away. It's one of those bland business hotels that could be anywhere in the world, but, as Dad says, they'll only really be sleeping there. For the first three days of their visit, Imogen and I are at school and Dad has to work, so Gran and Mrs. Allison do all the usual sightseeing things together. Gran has been to New York before, but it's Mrs. Allison's first visit to the Big Apple, and it's love at first bite. She adores all the dogs in their little quilted jackets, although she says they make her miss Sir Lancelot, who is staying with her sister in Essex.

Jen has invited all five of us to her house for Thanksgiving. I haven't seen her since the Halloween dance, although I often see Dash at school marching along in the junior kindergarten caterpillar formation. He's usually talking nonstop to whichever unfortunate child he has been partnered with that day. If Dash notices me, he stops dead, causing a pileup of four-year-olds behind him, and shouts hello, waving manically until I wave back.

"Why would Jen invite us for Thanksgiving?" I asked Dad when he told me. "Isn't it supposed to be a family holiday? We hardly know her."

"She's being nice, Kitty. She thought it would be fun

for us to experience an all-American Thanksgiving. I'm really looking forward to it."

"Why isn't she celebrating with her family?"

Dad sighed. "Her parents are visiting her brother and his wife in Seattle, so she invited us, and I've accepted her kind offer."

I don't think Gran is going to be thrilled about spending Thanksgiving with a random woman.

"Have you told Gran where we're going?"

"Yes, Kitty. I've told Eleanor we're going to a friend's house for Thanksgiving."

"Did you tell her it's a female friend?"

"I think she probably guessed that when I said the friend's name is Jennifer."

I raised an eyebrow. This is going to be interesting. Not much gets past Gran.

Jen and Dashiell live in a townhouse on West Tenth Street. The house is tall and thin, like its owner, and when Jen welcomes us inside, I'm not surprised to see that the walls are painted in shades of white, cream, taupe, and gray—all very tasteful and very bland. The only injections of color come from four huge canvases of fluorescent splatters, taller than me, that hang in the hallway and stick out like sore thumbs.

Jen is dressed from head to toe in neutrals like her home. She's wearing cream corduroy trousers, and a soft-looking silk shirt in palest peach. Her makeup is barely visible, just a hint of shimmer on her cheekbones and a glossy nude lip shade that I know Imogen will be coveting. She greets us all warmly and, ignoring my frosty vibes and Gran's outstretched hand, hugs us both. Mrs. Allison, who doesn't have any of Gran's physical boundaries or my animosity, embraces Jen vigorously and is delighted when Dashiell flings his arms around her legs. Dashiell is an explosion of color to rival the abstract paintings. He's dressed in purple trousers and an apple-green T-shirt, that reads "Far Out, Brussels Sprout!" in white letters. He leaps around in excitement like a badly trained puppy, which other people seem to find charming, but I find obnoxious. I'm pretty sure Gran feels the same way.

We follow Jen downstairs to an enormous kitchen, which, despite the clinical stainless steel appliances and glossy white marble surfaces, feels friendlier than the rooms upstairs. The cavernous fridge has Dash's artwork taped to it, and the large wooden table is candlelit and decorated with miniature pumpkins and turkey place settings. Jen notices me looking at them in surprise and laughs.

"Holiday-themed tables are my guilty pleasure, Kitty," she says. "You should see my Fourth of July picnic set—all stars and stripes. Jonathan, my husband, used to hide the holiday editions of home decor magazines to keep me from buying anything else!"

Dad had told us that Jonathan had died in a car accident before Dash was born. This seemed like too intimate a thing for me to know about Jen, but then I realized she must know all about my mum, given that she and Dad had been chatting on Flying Solo. I don't want her to know about my family's deepest darkest moments, but I do feel sorry for anyone who has lost someone they love, whether shockingly quickly on a dark, icy road or agonizingly slowly in a bright hospital room.

Death is death, and grief is grief. I shake my head to dislodge the unwelcome images.

One of the best things about today is that there are no Mum-associated memories. We won't all be sitting here thinking "this time last year" like we will at Christmas or New Year's or birthdays. In England, Thanksgiving is just another Thursday in November. Jessica will be doing her homework. Kate and Matt will still be at work. Sam will be with a patient in his office. Cleo, who has Gran's next-door neighbor popping in to feed her, will probably be napping.

"It all looks very festive, dear," says Mrs. Allison, setting down the apple crumble she made in our kitchen this morning along with a container of homemade custard and a plate of chocolate chip cookies on the counter.

"You're the cake lady," Dash says. "I've seen you on TV."

"The cake lady? I like that. I could use that for the title of my cookbook. Aren't you a clever boy? Let's try these cookies later and see if they're half as sweet as you."

"I'm clever and adorable," says Dash, smiling winningly.

Mrs. Allison is officially a television star. She was voted fan favorite on the BBC website at the end of her season of *The Great British Bake Off*, and is a "hot commodity," according to Barry, the agent who now represents her. Barry also manages numerous C-list celebrities' careers, most of them from reality TV shows like *Big Brother* and *The X Factor*. Mrs. Allison has appeared on a handful of morning television programs and is in the middle of writing a cookbook of her favorite recipes. Her season of *The Great British Baking Show*, as it's called here, is now on American TV. Dashiell wants to take her into school for show-and-tell.

"I'm hoping the BBC will invite me to be on *Strictly*

Come Dancing. Barry says it's a real possibility. Apparently, the public finds me very relatable," Mrs. Allison says.

"That episode you made me watch was dreadful, Elizabeth. I don't know why you'd want to go on it. There isn't even any baking, just a bunch of washed-up celebrities and former politicians making fools of themselves doing the fox-trot and the cha-cha. Are you sure you can dance? Don't forget, I've seen you at Zumba."

"We have that show here, but it's called *Dancing with the Stars*," Jen says quickly as she tries to gloss over Gran's Zumba insult. Maybe Dad warned her about Gran and Mrs. Allison's bickering.

"Well, there were certainly no stars on the version I saw," mutters Gran.

"It's a brilliant way to lose weight. All the celebs look marvelous by the end of the season. I'd be the envy of the Zumba girls," says Mrs. Allison. "Mind you, I'm not going to worry about my waistline just before this scrumptious-looking lunch."

"Henry told me his dad was asked to go on that show," I say without thinking.

"Who's Henry?" asks Mrs. Allison.

"It's Kitty's boyfriend," says Imogen. "His dad is that famous actor, James Davenport."

"James Davenport is a bit of all right," says Mrs. Allison.

"He really is," says Jen. "I've seen him at school a few times. Very handsome, especially if you like brooding vibes."

"Henry is not my boyfriend!"

"Well, if I ever were to consider having another man in my life, he would be on the list. I swore off men after Mr. Allison broke my heart," she explains to Jen.

"He's a bit young for you, Mrs. A.," says Imogen.

"Age is just a number, dear."

"Henry is not my boyfriend," I repeat, wishing I'd never mentioned the Davenport family. I should have known Imogen would jump at the chance to embarrass me.

"Whatever you say, Kitty," says my sister, with a smug look on her face.

"Bon appetit!" says Mrs. Allison.

After an enormous lunch, I'm beginning to think I'll need to go on a ballroom dancing show. I ate a pile of turkey, a mountain of creamy mashed potatoes, three types of stuffing (sausage and apple, chestnut and cornbread, and sage and onion), a weird-looking but delicious-tasting green bean casserole that was precisely the same color as Henry's eyes, buttery sautéed carrots, cranberry sauce, pumpkin pie, and a slice of Mrs. Allison's apple crumble with custard. I did say no to a chocolate chip cookie.

"The average Thanksgiving meal is a whopping three thousand calories," says Dad, leaning back in his chair. "I think I ate twice that. Thank you so much, Jen, for a delicious lunch and for inviting us to join you on this special day. Happy Thanksgiving, everyone!"

Dad raises his glass of red wine, and Jen, Gran, and Mrs. Allison do the same. Imogen and Dash toast with sparkling apple juice, and after a poke in the side, I raise my glass too.

"Hear, hear!" says Mrs. Allison. "Rob, I thought your trousers looked tight before we even started eating. I'm surprised you were able to fit a big lunch in there."

Dad looks embarrassed. "They're skinny. It's the style."

"That might be the in thing, but I came prepared to enjoy my lunch by wearing an elastic waistband." Mrs. Allison twangs the elastic playfully, winking at Dad, who looks mortified, while Jen tries not to laugh.

When the dishwasher is humming away and the immaculate kitchen is even more immaculate than it was when we arrived, Jen turns on the American football game, apparently a Thanksgiving tradition even though nobody seems interested in watching it. Gran and Mrs. Allison are dozing in armchairs, Imogen is glued to her phone, and Dash has fallen asleep on the sofa, his head on my dad's lap. I suddenly feel a pang for the father who never got to meet his little boy. He should be here cuddling up with his son on the sofa after Thanksgiving lunch. Instead, there are five random people from England celebrating a holiday that isn't theirs with his wife and child. I wonder if Jen is thinking the same thing.

There are photos of her husband, Jonathan, dotted around the house. A few are taped onto the fridge, and others are framed on the walls. He has the same dark eyes, olive skin, and soft-looking curls as his son. There's a picture of him and Jen in front of a waterfall, both of them grinning from ear to ear. Another photo is taken on a beach with impossibly white sand and a sea so blue it looks photoshopped. Jen is wearing a cream strappy dress with a pink-tinged orchid tucked behind one ear, and Jonathan is in a pale-blue shirt and linen trousers. Both of them are barefoot and perfect.

"Our wedding day," she told me when she saw me looking at the photo.

When Imogen and I discuss the photos later, she is adamant that Jonathan's appearance should put my mind at rest about any future romance between Dad and Jen.

"Did you see how good-looking her husband was? She's definitely out of Dad's league."

"He's not any better-looking than Dad," I say loyally. "Jonathan's just a different type."

"Yeah, the hot type."

CHAPTER TWENTY-TWO

PONYTAIL GIRL STRIKES BACK

A week after Thanksgiving, I'm sitting at the kitchen table studying for a science quiz when Imogen flounces into the apartment and marches through to her room, slamming the door so hard that a picture on the wall wobbles. Dad and I share a "teenagers, what are you going to do" shrug, and I continue with my homework. Dad calls out a few times to tell Imogen that supper is ready, but when there's no response, he sighs and apologetically sends me into the lion's den to fetch her. Her bedroom is in darkness, but I can see her outline on the bed; she's lying on her side facing the wall.

"What's up, Imo?" I ask, sitting down. Surprisingly, she doesn't tell me to leave like she usually does. "Did someone spit on your shoes again?"

"No," she says in a shaky voice and throws a ripped-up

Polaroid of Josh over her shoulder and bursts into tears.

"Girls," shouts Dad from the kitchen. "Supper, now!"

"Hang on," I tell Imogen and slide back down the hall-way to the kitchen.

"Dad, we have a situation back there—Josh drama, I think. It's an emotional code red. I'll call you for backup if I need it."

"What about supper?" Dad says.

"You eat. Imo needs me."

I feel unusually competent as I swish back to her room. Imogen, reluctantly at first, agrees I can switch on her bedside lamp, and with much sniffing tells me that Lily texted her to say she'd spotted Josh in Star-bucks with Scarlett Wilson after school.

"The one in Belsize Park, Kitty. Our Starbucks!"

I wonder what Josh and Scarlett ordered, but as Imo-gen bursts into a fresh round of sobs, I decide that it doesn't really matter whether they had tall hot choco-lates or venti caramel Frappuccinos.

"Did they have the drinks to go?" I ask instead.

"Kitty, what has that got to do with anything?"

"Well, if they got them to go, then they could have just run into each other there."

"Well, they didn't get them to go," she says in a little-girl voice, which I think is supposed to be an impression of me. "They sat down at the table by the window. That's how Lily saw them. Everyone will have seen them. It's so embarrassing. And they had cake pops!"

Again, it enters my head to ask what flavor, but that is definitely irrelevant, so I just pat Imogen's shoulder and try and fail to think of something helpful to say. My brief reign as an eloquent and empathetic supporter of my sister is over as quickly as it began.

The patting must be getting annoying since Imogen pulls away from my hand.

"Just go, Kitty," she says, the sound of heartbreak cracking her voice.

I tiptoe out of her room, closing the door as gently as I can.

The next morning there's no sign of Imogen in the kitchen when I go through for breakfast, yawning and rubbing my eyes. She's usually showered, fragrant, and perfectly dressed by the time I drag myself out of bed.

"Has Imo already gone to school?" I ask Dad.

"She's not feeling great. I said she could take a mental health day."

"Did she tell you about Josh?"

"She did. I saw her light on late last night, so I went in to see her. She was crying, poor love. She's far too good for him anyway."

I feel a wave of fondness for Dad. The indignation

that someone would dare to betray his daughter has him bristling with outrage.

"I'll go in and say goodbye then."

I knock gently on Imogen's door, but there's no answer. I peek into the room and see that she's fallen asleep with a book in her hand and the light still on. I tiptoe in to pick it up and lay it down on her bedside table. The story is one we both cherished when we were small, *The Little White Horse*, by Elizabeth Goudge. Our copy is well thumbed, the cover faded and velvety to the touch from dozens of readings. The story of Maria Merryweather and the magical Moonacre Manor is as familiar to me as a long-lost friend. I know that for Imogen, reading this will have been like a warm bath to help her sleep. I'm sure she wouldn't want me to know she's been reading it. It's too babyish. I didn't even know it came to New York with us. I wonder where she keeps it and what other books she brought with her. I imagine a box at the bottom of her closet filled with comfort books starring brave and resourceful girls: Heidi, Pippi Longstocking, and Katy. Imogen reads for comfort the way someone else might binge on ice cream, or I might open tester jars of paint. I turn off the lamp and tiptoe out of the room.

The next day Imogen drags herself back to school, but her usually gleaming hair is pulled into a dull, messy bun, and she has dark circles under her eyes. Dad looks helplessly at me as Imogen pushes a piece of toast around her plate before shuffling off to the subway station.

"How long is she going to be like this?" I ask Dad.

"I'm not sure, Kitty. This is one of those times I feel totally useless. Mum would have known exactly what to do."

Dad saying that makes me think of his WWLD online self, looking for advice.

"Did you google it?" I ask.

He hadn't, so we do, and scan articles about teen breakups: "Ten Dos and Don'ts when Helping Your Brokenhearted Teen."

"Oh, great," sighs Dad, reading the *don'ts* section. "I think I did all these things. Don't say, 'You'll get over it soon.' I did. Don't make it about you—I told her about Charlotte Carter."

I raise my eyebrows.

"I was fifteen. It was devastating." He continues reading. "Don't dis the ex, well I did that!"

"Oops, I did that too. I called Josh a loser," I admit.

"Well, he is a loser! I'm not sure about this advice, Kitty. I think all we need to do is listen."

"I can actually hear Mum saying that to you. 'Just listen, Rob. You don't need to fix this, just be there.'"

"Gosh, you're right."

Dad heads off to work muttering his new mantra, "listen, be there, don't fix, listen, be there, don't fix," under his breath. Dad and I seem to be figuring out WWLD together.

Early that afternoon, I track down Henry during our free period. He grins when he sees me approaching. We haven't chatted much since before Thanksgiving, but he's just the person I need to help me cheer up Imogen.

"Henry, I need a favor."

"Sure, what's up? Considering that you get better grades than me in almost every subject, I hope it isn't homework."

"It's not. It's an art project. Would you mind doing the drawings for a story I've written for my sister? I want it to be a comic strip, but I can only do the words, not the pictures."

Henry looks intrigued, so I sit down next to him and explain Josh/Scarlett-gate. I talk him through the *Ponytail Girl* story line, and his smile broadens with every word.

"Cool idea. Of course I'll help."

Henry brings Ponytail Girl to life in all her glory. He uses colored pencils to draw Imogen/Ponytail Girl's gleaming golden hair. Scarlett Wilson is portrayed with frizzy red hair; she always claimed it was strawberry blond. She also has terrible split ends and a simultaneously sulky and smug expression on her face.

"Wow, it's as if you'd met her!" I tell him.

I pull up a picture of Josh on Instagram, and Henry perfectly captures Floppy Hair Boy, who Ponytail Girl has to rescue after he and Scarlett fall backward into a surprisingly deep duck pond in Regent's Park while taking a selfie. As a bedraggled Josh sits looking dejected on a park bench with pondweed in his hair, Scarlett is chased into the distance by a flock of angry geese. Ponytail Girl walks off into the sunset, alone but not lonely and absolutely magnificent. It's a work of genius. I ask Henry to scribble his initials next to mine in the corner of the page. Creating a comic strip wasn't in the *dos* for helping someone get over breakups, and it doesn't fit in with the "just listen" plan, but I have a feeling it might make Imogen smile. Maybe not today, but soon.

"My turn to ask you for a favor," Henry says.

"English homework?" I ask.

"Nope. Hair dye."

"You want me to dye your hair for you?"

"No, dummy. I want you to help me pick out a color."

"Me?"

"Yes, Kitty, you. Will you, queen of all colors,

accompany me on a treacherous journey to a magical kingdom called Duane Reade? There you will help me select a potion to transform this London Stone,"—Henry ruffles his hair—"into a wondrous shade of green."

"You're kind of a dork," I tell him, not unkindly.

"I know," he says, smiling. "All the best people are. See you by the gate at three-thirty." And he strolls off down the hallway.

I go into the bathroom to think about whether Henry or anyone else would consider a trip to Duane Reade to choose green hair dye as constituting a date. Having spent my entire life at a girls' school, I'm not used to having boys as friends. Ava is friends with tons of the boys in our grade, but they hang out in a group, not in pairs, plus they've known each other since they were about four. Dylan and Mimi are the only official couple. Everyone calls them Milan or Dimi, which they strangely don't seem to mind. I don't want to be called Kenry or Hitty.

As I wash my hands, I examine myself in the mirror. My bob has grown out, and the ends of my hair almost brush my shoulders. My face is thinner than it was; my chubby cheeks have melted away over the last six months, revealing a hidden feature of my mum's beneath them. It turns out that I have her cheekbones. My nose still has its distinctive bump that I wish I could shave off. I touch the smattering of friendly freckles that stay there year-round, even when their summer cousins have long since faded away, and consider what Imogen would do. If she wanted to go and help a boy pick out some green hair dye, she would, and she wouldn't care what anyone thought about it. Fine, I'll try the Imogen way. I swish my nonexistent ponytail and head to class.

Despite my attempts to be cool and not care if anyone sees me with Henry, I am a nervous wreck until we get safely inside Duane Reade. I decided the best plan would be to race out of school ahead of anyone else and hope Henry came out quickly. Miraculously, he was already at the gates when I got there, and we managed to get the five blocks from school to Duane Reade without spotting anyone we know. Maybe he didn't want to be seen with me either.

Henry navigates expertly to the aisle for hair color. There are hundreds of shades to choose from. Most of the boxes have pictures of women on the front, but it doesn't seem to bother Henry. I see a box with a photo of a girl who looks a lot like Imogen on the front. The blond color is named California Dreamin'. It annoys me that they have dropped the g. I'm about to comment on this to Henry, but decide I might sound like a geek, so keep it to myself.

"Here's the color I used last time," Henry says, passing me a box.

"Blue Steel?" I laugh, reading the front.

"I didn't choose it based on the name, Kitty. Come on, help me look for green."

"Why green?"

"It's almost Christmas. I always do green at Christmas."

"How festive," I say, perusing the boxes of green. Unsurprisingly, there's a limited selection. I examine colors called Emerald City and Appletini before handing him Enchanted Forest.

"Nice," he says. "Thanks, Kitty."

"They should give the colors better names," I tell him.

"What would you call this one?"

"Frog's Brow."

Henry laughs and shakes his head.

"And I'm the dork?" he says.

CHAPTER TWENTY-THREE

IMOGEN'S ICE CREAM

By the end of the following week, Imogen is still in a foul mood and only managed a small smile when I presented her with the *Ponytail Girl* comic strip. She pushes food mournfully around her plate, sighs over her homework, and every night when I sneak into her room to turn off her light, she's holding a different comfort book in her hand.

"I want to go home," she announces over dinner.

"That's supposed to be Kitty's line," says Dad, looking concerned. "I thought you loved New York, Imogen."

"I did, but I've had enough. I'm ready to go back to London."

"Don't let Josh spoil the last few weeks for you," Dad says.

Imogen puts down her fork, pushes back her chair, and stands up.

"It's not about Josh. He's a total loser anyway."

"We all agree with that," I say to her back as she stalks off to her room.

I hate Josh. How dare he treat my sister this way? How dare he make her feel bad about herself? She's worth a hundred of him. He's lucky she ever even bothered to speak to him, let alone go out with him.

"Dad, I want to do something nice for Imogen to cheer her up."

"What are you thinking of, love?"

"Well, I know you said we couldn't paint the apartment, but how about I paint just one wall of Imogen's room? I promise I'll help paint it white again when it's time to go."

Dad looks dubious. "It's a nice idea, Kitty, but it's not very practical. We're only here for another few weeks. How about you get her some chocolates or flowers?"

"But I want to do this," I say stubbornly. "I want to make Imogen a special color of her own. I read about this place where you can make your own paint. You take in a swatch of fabric or something, and they can match the color."

Dad looks thoughtful. I wonder if he's pondering what Mum would do. "Okay, why not? What color are you going to make for her?"

I close my eyes and think back to one of my earliest

memories of my sister. She and I are standing on a pebbly beach eating ice cream out of cones, probably somewhere in Dorset. The wind is whipping Imogen's ponytail into the vanilla ice cream that I'm clutching in my chubby hand. Her ice cream is ponytail free. I used to think about colors even then, and I remember noticing how the creamy vanilla treat was the same color as the palest blond streaks in my sister's ponytail.

"You know the lightest part of Imogen's hair. The strands that are the same color as vanilla ice cream?"

"I can't say that I do," Dad says.

"Well, that's the color."

"You can't snip off a piece of her hair," Dad says. "She's upset enough as it is. What are you going to do? Take a tub of vanilla ice cream to the paint store?"

"That's exactly what I'm going to do," I tell him, grinning. "I'm going to turn ice cream into paint."

As it turns out, making your own paint is extraordinarily simple. The DIY store has an ingenious device called a spectrophotometer that's about the size of a shoebox and measures color electronically. The guy operating it, whose name tag reads Mike, shines a light onto the ice cream we brought with us in a cooler to stop it from melting.

"The machine takes a reading of each wavelength of

light reflected off the object," Mike explains. "I've never matched ice cream before. I hope it doesn't melt and mess up my equipment."

"What do people usually bring in for you to match?" Dad asks.

"All sorts of things. The woman before you had a Tiffany jewelry box. Someone once brought in their dog."

"Really? Did you match it?" I ask. What an amazing discovery! I assume Kate knows all about the spectrophotometer, but I'll tell her about it just in case she doesn't.

"Yes." Mike nods. "It works about ninety percent of the time."

"What about the other ten percent?" Dad asks, looking at me nervously. He knows we'll be here until the color is perfect.

"Easy, if it looks a bit off, we just add some blue, red, white, whatever is needed, until it's right."

Thirty minutes later and after learning about visible light being measured in nanometers, one of which is equal to a billionth of a meter, the color is a perfect match for the now gloopy ice cream.

"I can save the formula on file for you in case you need to order more. I just need a name for it," says Mike.

"Imogen's Ice Cream, Kitty's Color, Number One," I say. "Each word capitalized, please."

"We usually just do the last name of the person ordering it," Mike says, but dutifully types in the name of my
very first paint. Would you believe, creating a bespoke
color with the spectrophotometer costs the same as buying regular, ready-mixed paint?

"Why wouldn't everyone do this?" I ask Dad as we lug
the paint home.

"Kitty, did you see how many color paints they had in
there? Hundreds, maybe thousands. I think most people
assume that someone else has already invented the perfect shade."

Well, most people are wrong. There are so many more
colors than anyone could ever invent. Exact shades exist
only because that person sees it in that way on that particular day. A lifetime of experiences, a million different
types of light, their mood when they see it, all swirl
together to create a unique color that may only exist for
a split second, just like Imogen and the ice cream. Now
that color is captured for eternity, thanks to Mike and
his marvelous spectrophotometer.

I decided it best not to consult my sister before painting
her wall, in case she said no. She has a two-night school
trip to Washington, DC, this week, and Dad agrees
that's the best time to paint. After much pleading, he
agrees that I can miss a day of school, just this once. I

put on a pair of old jeans and one of Dad's T-shirts, tie my hair back into what is a slightly less stubby ponytail now that it's grown out, and we begin. We moved the furniture away from the wall, wiped it down, and put on the primer last night, so we're ready to go. I pop open the tin of paint using a palette knife, and it makes the most satisfying sound as it opens, revealing the buttery interior. Dipping the broad paintbrush into the velvety paint feels delicious. It even smells like ice cream, but that could be my imagination. Dad says it smells like paint and that I have to stop sniffing it. The wall comes to life as with each stroke of glossy paint, a gentle beam of sunshine appears in its place. We finish just as the sun is beginning to dip, and the pale vanilla takes on a golden sheen.

The final touch is an enlarged copy of the photo of Imogen and me on the Dorset beach, which I've put into a frame and placed on her desk. I look at our faces— Imogen is smiling straight into the camera, and I'm looking at my ice cream, anxious to keep it safe from the ponytail.

"What if she doesn't like it, Dad?" I ask, examining the wall nervously.

"She'll love it," he says.

★ ★ ★

When Imogen gets back from her trip, we are in the kitchen waiting for her.

"Kitty's got a surprise for you, Imogen. Lead the way, Kitty," says Dad.

I open the door to Imogen's room and step aside to let her walk in first.

"I invented this color for you. I hope you like it. It's called Imogen's Ice Cream."

Imogen stares at the wall, then heads to her desk and picks up the photo of us on the beach.

"Imogen's Ice Cream," I repeat stupidly.

"Kitty, I love it," she says, rushing over to where I'm standing in the doorway and pulling me into a hug. After a few seconds, I break free, blushing.

"It's perfect," she says. "Did I ever tell you that you're a fab sister?" she asks, grinning at me.

"Nope."

"Well, you are."

Imogen gives me another hug, and as she steps away, she flicks her ponytail with some of her old flair. I leave the room, my cheeks warm with pride. I can see my sister's powers returning with every swing of her ponytail. You can't keep a good superhero down.

CHAPTER TWENTY-FOUR

GLITTER EVERYWHERE

Overnight the storeowners of Manhattan replace their giant turkey and pumpkin window displays with stars, trees, Santas, and Menorahs. Henry was right; the glitter on the decorations that appear in the school's hallways does seem to get everywhere. Ava's mum is once again in charge of decorations. Ava says that the other parents find it annoying that her mum always runs the show, but they probably think it's easier to fall in her mom's decorating wake than to try to start their own tide.

"It's time for her to get a job. It's been fifteen years since she stopped working at the magazine when my brother was born," Ava complains. "Then maybe she'd stop interfering in my life."

The PTA team quickly transforms hallways, the gym,

and classrooms into snow-filled palaces. Winter Wonderland is the theme of this year's Winterfest, and Ava's mum tells me that Narnia is her inspiration.

"Isn't that going to be a bit frightening for the younger kids?" I ask her.

"It's not a literal interpretation, Kitty. There isn't going to be a White Witch trying to kill children and hobbits."

"I think you mean fauns. Mr. Tumnus is half man, half goat. The hobbits are in Lord of the Rings." Even as I say this, I know that I sound like a brat. I'm still mad at her for saying we lost Mum.

"Anyway," she says, ignoring me, "Narnia is the inspiration. The most direct reference to it is the streetlamp we've installed outside Principal Carter's office."

She hands me a bag of fake snow, which she instructs me to scatter around the base of the lamppost.

The Lion, the Witch and the Wardrobe was one of my favorite books to read with Mum. On the cover of the copy I have, there's a picture of Peter, Susan, Edmund, and Lucy pushing their way through huge fur coats in the wardrobe. The idea of a normal world behind me and an enchanted one in front was mesmerizing, and I spent many happy afternoons recreating this scene in Mum's wardrobe. Obviously, she didn't have any fur coats, but some of her longer dresses felt nice to burrow through before I bumped into the oak back of the cupboard.

As I pile the snow carefully around the base of the lamppost, I find one of those secret piles of grief glitter Gran told me about when I remember an illustration from the book. The lion, Aslan, was tied to a stone table, his magnificent mane shorn. Mum's hair had started falling out in clumps when she began chemo, so she'd asked Dad to shave it all off one day. She had the most beautifully shaped head, and Dad used to kiss it whenever he walked past her. Some days she wore scarves or hats when we went out, but mostly she would walk around the neighborhood with her bald head held high. People used to give us sad, sympathetic looks, and told their children not to stare. Mum would wave at the kids, her smile as radiant as the therapy that was making her feel so ill.

"They think I'm one of them, Kitty!" she said delightedly. "An oversize baby with a bald head." She waved at a baby sitting in his stroller, who gave her a gummy grin in return and opened and closed his chubby hand back at her. He seemed delighted with his ability to control his hand movements and got distracted, waving at himself.

In the story, of course, Aslan doesn't die. His golden

mane grows back, and with a roar to wake the spring, he breaks the chains holding him to the stone table and leaps off it to freedom. Mum's golden hair never grew back, and the cancer chains holding her were unbreakable. Spring never came. But still, when I think of this, I see Mum giggling as she waves at the baby, and that makes me smile a bit too. Maybe the glitter can hide flecks of happiness as well as sadness. I turn to the supply box and pull out a jar of gold glitter, sprinkling it carefully onto the snow.

The day of the Winterfest is my last ever day at school in New York. It never felt real to me that I was a student here—more as if I had come for a day's visit to experience a completely different school and then got stuck. Ava has organized a goodbye party for me during homeroom. She has clearly inherited her mum's event planning skills and has decorated my desk with Union Jacks and Stars and Stripes. There are cupcakes with little flags stuck into the frosting and a big card that everyone has signed, even Principal Carter. Ava has put her hair into a bun today and pushed the mini flags into her shiny hair, making it look a bit like she has stuck a cupcake on top of her head. Surely even she can't have planned that? I decide not to ask her.

I had volunteered to work at the carnival in the gym at the Winterfest. Henry is doing the same shift as me on the hook-a-duck stall. I can't say this is a coincidence considering I had carefully checked the sign-up sheet for his name before surreptitiously adding my own with a blush. It has crossed my mind more than once that I might miss Henry when I leave New York.

"This is my regular gig," he says. "Third year in a row."

"You must enjoy it."

"Not really, I just can't be bothered to try anything else. Mom gave me a T-shirt for my birthday that says 'APATHY . . . I can take it or leave it.'"

"That's pretty funny. I wish I could be so laid-back. My godmother, Kate, once sent me a card that said 'Today is the tomorrow you worried about yesterday' on the front. The problem is that when you know the absolute worst thing can happen, then it's hard not to imagine everything else going wrong." I realize it's the first time I've said that out loud.

Henry nods as if he understands.

Principal Carter walks past the stall and waves at us. He's wearing a Santa hat and beard. I try and fail to imagine Mrs. Brooks dressed as Father Christmas.

"Ho, ho, ho, very festive!" Principal Carter says, pointing at Henry's hair, which is now Enchanted Forest green, a brighter version of his green-bean-colored eyes.

"Thanks," says Henry. "Nice beard."

As Principal Carter passes, Dad, Jen, Imogen, and Dash appear in front of the stall.

"Hi," I say, hoping they'll move on before I need to introduce Henry.

"Can I have a ducky, please," asks Dash, holding out a token in payment.

"I'll take one too, Kitty," says Dad.

"Me three," says Imogen.

Oh, great!

"Here you go," says Henry, appearing at my shoulder like an unsummoned genie, proffering ducks. "I'm Henry."

"Henry," says Imogen knowingly, "how nice to meet you. I'm Kitty's sister, Imogen. We've heard a lot about you."

"Oh, really?" Henry looks surprised. "I guess I've heard a lot about you too, Ponytail Girl."

It's Imogen's turn to look surprised.

"The comic strip," Henry explains. "I did the drawings."

Dad and Jen say hi, and I notice Jen looking around

furtively, presumably to see if James Davenport is anywhere nearby. Imogen has three more turns on the hook-a-duck stall to annoy me before I tell her that the game is really for the under-tens, and she flounces off, swinging her glossy mane.

"Ponytail Girl was pretty good at hooking ducks," Henry says.

"Oh, Imogen's good at everything," I say, scowling after her.

"You're pretty good at everything too, except state capitals. When are you going back to London?"

"New Year's Day."

"Too bad you won't be here next semester," he says. "I guess you're looking forward to getting home."

"I guess. It's like I pressed pause on my life in London, wandered off for a bit, and am about to hit play again."

Henry laughs. "Well, if you're ever back in New York, maybe you can stop by school and say hi?"

"You should come to London on holiday," I say. "Perhaps your dad will have a movie premiere there, and you can take Imogen with you as your date. She's always wanted to go on the red carpet."

"Thanks, Kitty. Your sister's cute but not my type," Henry says, studying me closely.

I blush and fumble with the duck I'm trying to unhook. Maybe I'm supposed to ask what his type is? Instead, I change the subject to his hair color—apparently, next up is pink for Valentine's Day. Once we've finished packing away the ducks, we drop the takings from the stall at the secretary's office.

"You headed for the subway?" Henry asks.

"No. I'm meeting Dad and Imo at Jen's house for a goodbye dinner with her and Dash." I roll my eyes and sigh theatrically. Henry knows I am not a fan of Jen or Dash.

"Well, see you, then."

Henry pulls me into a soft, clumsy hug and places the whisper of a kiss on my cheek.

"Bye, Kitty."

"Bye, Henry."

I smile a small secret smile all the way to Jen's house, my warm cheek tingling softly where Henry's kiss had fallen. Does a kiss on the cheek count as a first kiss from a boy? I'll have to ask Jess. Not that she'd know. I'd like to ask Imogen, but she'd laugh at me. The best person to ask would be Mum. As it is, I'll hug the secret to myself all the way back to London and my old/new life.

CHAPTER TWENTY-FIVE

A VERY WHITE CHRISTMAS

Christmas in New York is like a scene from a movie. Snow has begun to fall, delicate flakes sticking to my coat, the final special effect to complete the picture-perfect backdrop. Stalls selling Christmas trees have sprung up every few blocks, and Imogen and I manage to convince Dad to drag a tree home with us, even though it's only a week until we're moving back to London. Imogen wants a tall, elegant tree, but I notice a stubby one with unattractively knobbly top branches tucked behind its more glamorous siblings.

"Dad, please can we get this one?" I say, placing a gloved hand protectively on its branches.

"Kitty, why do you want the ugliest tree?" Imogen asks.

"I feel sorry for it."

My sister snorts in derision and looks at Dad.

"I'll let you have it for half price," the stall owner says, sensing an opportunity to off-load this spruce pariah.

"Sold!" says Dad, who had been grumbling about spending money on a tree, and had already told us that apart from lights, he wouldn't be buying any decorations since we have three boxes full in the attic in London. It's always been one of my favorite parts of Christmas when Dad gets the boxes down and we sit and unwrap them, releasing them from their creased tissue-paper bedding. Seeing them again is like meeting long-lost friends. There are red, gold, and green shiny baubles, a set of crocheted reindeer bought from a craft fair, a host of tiny gold angels with intricate trumpets and harps, white glittery snowflakes, a family of sweet gray feathery owls, and two grinning Father Christmases made lovingly by Imogen and me out of toilet paper tubes when we were younger.

We go to buy lights, well, Dad does while Imogen and I stand outside the store holding the tree, and I scowl at anyone who looks at it disparagingly. It really is an ugly thing. Faced with the disdain of other shoppers who no doubt have perfect trees, Imogen becomes protective of it. She swings her superhero ponytail and glares at them, one arm defensively wrapped around its twisted branches. I grin at her, and she swishes her hair at me too.

By the time we get home, the snow is falling hard. Looking out of the window on the twenty-fourth floor, it feels like I'm in a snow globe that someone has shaken. Dad winds the lights around the tree, tests them, and unlike our lights at home, they all work the first time. Imogen and I bake star-shaped lemon cookies to hang on the tree and make paper garlands, while Dad pours himself a generous glass of ruby-red wine and turns on Christmas music. We work away in silence while Frank Sinatra instructs us to have ourselves a merry little Christmas. We stand back to examine our handiwork. Despite the lights and the star cookies, the tree still looks a bit sad.

"Hang on," says Dad, rustling around in the bag the lights were in and producing a cardboard box. "I think we need this."

"But you said no decorations," Imogen says.

"I know, I know, but I saw this in the store. She was the last one. I couldn't leave her there—you'll see."

I squeeze Dad's hand and open the box. Inside, nestling in tissue paper, is a delicate-looking fairy. She has a sweet, familiar painted face, a cloud of golden hair, white sparkling skirts, and gossamer wings. The fairy looks a little like Mum on their wedding day—minus the wings, of course. Dad places her gently on top of the tree. We switch on the tree lights, turn off all the lights in the apartment, and sit looking at the delicate fairy, holding court from the top of the misshapen tree with its home-made decorations and cheap white icicle-shaped lights. It's perfect. Mum would have loved it.

When I wake on Christmas morning, all is calm, all is quiet, and all is white. The snow has settled on the ground, and the sky is a deliciously rich blue. In fact, the sky is the same shade as it was on our first day of sight-seeing in New York, St Giles Blue, color number 280. I don't think England ever has an August sky in Decem-ber. When I was little, I used to love to sneak downstairs before anyone else was awake to see if Father Christmas had eaten his slice of Christmas cake and Rudolph had munched his carrot. I realized embarrassingly late that it was Dad eating them, but we still used to leave them out every Christmas Eve. Last night is the first time we didn't. When I walk into the kitchen, Dad is sitting at the table, gazing into his cup of tea. There's a small pile of brightly colored and badly wrapped presents under the tree. Poor Dad, he would have had to wrap them all himself. He's terrible at gift wrapping. Usually, it was only his present to Mum that looked as if it had been savaged by Cleo. All the rest had neatly folded corners and were tied up with ribbon that Mum used to curl with scissors. The idea of Dad wrapping presents on his own is heartbreaking, if a broken heart can be broken again. I suppose it can, just like an arm or a leg.

"Daddy," I say, running over to him and climbing in his lap, using the name for him I abandoned when I was seven and Imogen started calling him Dad.

"Merry Christmas, love," he whispers into my hair.

"Happy Christmas," Imogen calls, appearing from her bedroom. "Race you to the presents, Kitty."

I stay in Dad's lap while Imogen goes and starts rummaging through the pile of presents, checking the gift tags for her name.

"Hang on," says Dad. "I have a special present for you both to open first."

He hands us each a small, impeccably wrapped box in glittery silver paper. Imogen's is tied with a deep violet bow and mine with a rich red one. There's a tag attached to the ribbon, and when I turn it over, my heart skips a beat. In Mum's lovely loopy writing, I read, "Merry Christmas, Kitty. Love, Mum and Dad xxx."

Inside my box is a charm, a tiny, perfect red ruby. Imogen's contains a miniature purple stone.

"They're your birthstones," Dad says. "An amethyst for Imogen and a ruby for Kitty. Mum wanted you to have something from both of us for your first Christmas without her."

I glance at Dad, who is looking from Imogen to me

with a worried expression on his face. Maybe he thinks we're going to start crying. Imogen is gazing into her box at her jewel. I study my tiny ruby. I want to ask Dad if Mum was the last person to touch it—had she been the one to put it into the box? I don't ask him, though. He looks so sad.

"I love it. Thank you. Can you help me put it on?"

Dad fumbles with the small clasp, his nails too short to get a grip. When it's attached, I nudge Imogen, who looks up from her box with a dazed expression. I fasten her charm for her, and we raise our wrists to each other as if toasting the gemstones, toasting our final Christmas present from Mum. I wonder what Imogen would want if she could have had any present from Mum at all. I know what I would have had—one last hug.

The rest of the day, we make an effort to jolly each other along, but there's a gaping hole. It's like a jigsaw puzzle missing the middle piece, which has disappeared between the floorboards, so there's no point ever doing the puzzle again. It will never be complete. The numbers don't add up. We are three-quarters of a family but feel like less than a half. You can't be safe on a chair with only three legs. Between the three of us, we do manage to make a haphazard Christmas lunch, which we then push around our plates. Dad forgot the potatoes and roast potatoes are my favorite part of the meal. The stuffing goes in the microwave and doesn't taste like Christmas, and we don't have brussels sprouts, as only Mum liked them, but the table looks wrong without them. As we're loading the dishwasher, I broach the subject.

"Can we have sprouts next year?" I ask Dad.

"Funny, I missed them too. Sorry, girls, not exactly a Christmas banquet."

"It was fine," Imogen said. "I'm glad we'll be back to Mrs. Allison's cooking soon. I bet she's having a delicious lunch. Was Gran going to her house?"

"No, Gran's gone to your great-aunt's house, and Mrs. A. is in Spain with her Zumba crew. What do you want to do now, girls? It's only two o'clock."

Imogen and I shrug, the day stretching ahead of us.

"I know," Dad says, a flash of inspiration and relief crossing his face. "We'll go ice skating."

"Will the rink be open on Christmas Day?" Imogen asks in surprise.

"Lots of things are open," Dad says. "It's not like in London, where everything closes for the day. Come on, let's wrap up warm and head out. It's our last week in New York, and we're not sitting around here moping all day. We'll go to the rink in Rockefeller Plaza. Your mum loved it there."

Despite the blue, blue sky, it is freezing outside. Only

in New York can people wear winter hats and sunglasses without looking crazy, but all thoughts of being cold melt away as I see the most enormous skyscraper of a Christmas tree.

"It's eighty feet tall," says Dad, "and there are eighteen thousand lights. Glad I didn't have to put those on!"

We swirl around on the ice hand in hand. Imogen is pink-cheeked and giggly, and we cling to each other as we spin around, laughing. I close my eyes and tilt my face up to the impossibly clear sky, feeling happier than I have all day. Dad watches us both grinning, and I wish Mum a silent Merry Christmas. I feel sure she's sitting on her star watching us and smiling.

On New Year's Eve, we finish packing up the apartment. It takes a surprisingly long time, and we seem to have accumulated an awful lot of stuff in four months.

"I'm going to have to pay for excess baggage," Dad groans, looking at Imogen's bags. "What on earth's in all these bags, Imogen?"

"Clothes," she says. "And makeup. And shoes."

We try to stay awake to watch the ball drop in Times Square but are all yawning by ten o'clock.

"Come on, girls, bed. We watched midnight in London. We saw Big Ben, so we can give the ball a miss. We've got an early flight in the morning."

At six a.m. on New Year's Day, I walk a loop of the apartment. It looks exactly as it did the first time we saw it. Even Imogen's Ice Cream has been painted over with a flat white emulsion. The sky is as blue as the day we arrived, but now the lawn below is blanketed with snow rather than sunbathers. The white walls wait silently for the next family. I'm ready to go home.

CHAPTER TWENTY-SIX

JANUARY BLUES

After the Technicolor extravaganza that is New York City, London seems gray and heavy. New York is a rambunctious toddler of a city, and London is a cantankerous old lady. The oldest building here is the Tower of London, built in 1080. Just imagine all the ghosts roaming the streets, soaking into the bricks and cobbles. Manhattan's oldest building is a mansion, built in 1765. If London were a character from a book, she'd be Miss Haversham from *Great Expectations*. New York would be Fudge from *Tales of a Fourth Grade Nothing*.

Our taxi ride from Heathrow Airport is the opposite of our hair-raising arrival in New York four months earlier. I gaze out of the window at the passing fields and trees. A visiting tourist on their way from the airport to the city would get a glimpse of the England of their dreams, before being plunged into a never-ending series of suburbs for the next hour. It's hard to know when you've arrived in London. In Manhattan, you either cross a bridge or emerge from a tunnel, and ta-da, you're there. It strikes me that I'll probably spend the coming months and possibly years comparing the two cities. I read a book once about a girl who had lived in England and India. She said that once you've lived in two countries, you never feel at home in either one.

When we get to Belsize Park, I do feel a shiver of happiness on seeing our friendly little house. Mrs. Allison and Gran are there to welcome us home with cups of tea and a pile of freshly baked scones and homemade raspberry jam.

"Gosh, don't you girls look grown-up. I'd hardly have recognized you, Kitty. Perhaps we need a trip to Marks & Spencer for you know what," Mrs. Allison says.

"It's only been a month since you saw me!" I say. "People go to Victoria's Secret in New York. There is no M&S there."

"No M&S," she says sadly. "Imagine that. All the wonderful shops they have in New York, but no M&S."

Imogen laughs. "Mrs. Allison, Kitty didn't need the first bra, let alone a second. If anything, her boobs are getting smaller. She's becoming concave!"

"Don't be horrid, Imogen. Anyway, what on earth is Victoria's Secret?" asks Gran.

"An underwear shop," I say.

"That doesn't sound at all appropriate for teenagers. Rob, do you know about this so-called Victoria's Secret?"

"It's fine, Gran," I say. "It's just like Gap except they only sell underwear and pajamas."

"Then I suggest you go to the Gap in future," says Gran, clearly picturing Victoria's Secret to be some terrible place. The way she says "the" Gap, with the emphasis on "the," makes me smile. I grin at her, and she smiles back at me. I've missed her so much.

Mrs. Allison is delighted with the dog jacket we bought for Sir Lancelot.

"Ooh, Sir Lancelot, won't you be elegant and toasty warm in this?" she says, struggling to squeeze his barrel of a body into the yellow-and-black tartan jacket.

"I told you he'd need an extra-large," mutters Dad as Sir Lancelot slobbers on his new shoes, part of his New York City wardrobe upgrade.

"Look, Rob, he missed you," Mrs. Allison says. "You know, it's funny because he doesn't usually like men, but he's never minded you."

Dad moves his spittle-covered shoe away from Sir Lancelot and looks offended, as if Sir Lancelot or Mrs. Allison, or maybe both of them, are questioning his masculinity. Cleo, who has been sitting on my lap purring, springs gracefully onto the counter, stepping neatly between the piles of mail and cups of tea. She watches Sir Lancelot from on high with a mixture of loathing and pity. Can cats roll their eyes? Cleo certainly seems to when she gets an uninterrupted view of Sir Lancelot stuffed into his new tartan jacket. He looks simultaneously comical and depressed. She averts her gaze and starts washing her already immaculate paws.

"Well, sorry to love you and leave you, but I need to adjust a recipe for my book. I've got an important meeting this week with my publisher," says Mrs. Allison.

Gran rolls her eyes and continues flicking through the book of *New Yorker* cartoons we bought for her. Mrs. Allison bustles off with Sir Lancelot, who looks frumpy in his new jacket. He has fat rolls bulging out of the leg, neck, and tail openings.

"That dog is getting obese," Gran says. "I'm sure she feeds him chocolate cakes and sticky toffee puddings. Girls, you should take him for a run in the park. The farthest Mrs. Allison walks him is up the street, and then they stop every few minutes for him to get a dog biscuit. Remember that time we took him out fundraising, Kitty? Once we got him up the hill, he started looking much perkier."

"Sir Lancelot can't run, Gran," I say. "He sometimes trots when he gets close to home or the butcher's shop, but he can't do that for long. It's difficult to get him all the way to the park because he's too heavy for me to carry onto the bus, and there's no way he can walk there and back."

"His legs are super short as well," says Imogen. "I bet Mrs. Allison wishes she'd chosen one of those cute little dogs that all the celebrities have that you can fit into your handbag. There were loads of those in New York."

Jess arrives later that afternoon. We squeal and jump up and down in the hallway for a few minutes before racing to my bedroom. Jess starts rummaging through my suitcase.

"You have the best clothes, Kitty," she sighs. "I need to borrow everything."

"Here you go, belated Christmas present." I hand her a Brandy Melville bag containing an identical hoodie to the one I'm wearing.

"I love it. Thanks!" Jess pulls it on immediately.

"What's been happening at school?" I ask.

Despite our weekly FaceTime calls, I feel disconnected from Jess and my old life. Haverstock Girls' School, Jess, Gran, Kate, Mrs. Allison, and Sam have all seemed weirdly separate and hazy while I've been in New York, as if I were trying to see them through a fogged-up windowpane. Jess regales me with stories of Mrs. Brooks' latest draconian dress code rule—no scrunchies permitted other than navy, black, or brown.

"Who even owns a brown scrunchie?" says Jess. "I'll tell you who; nobody, because it would be disgusting! My purple one was confiscated. I was supposed to get it back before the Christmas holiday, but the lost property was already locked up when I went to the office. My scrunchie wasn't lost property anyway; it was stolen."

I let Jessica's familiar voice wash over me. With every word she speaks, Henry, Ava, Jen, Dash, and my New York life seem further and further away. As they recede, London shifts into focus. It reminds me of when I went to the optician, and they kept flipping lenses down to see which one worked best.

"Here's your present, by the way," Jess says, handing me a small parcel. Inside is a lavender heart pillow the size of the palm of my hand. "I made it for you. Do you remember making them at school when we were little?" she asks, studying my face.

Of course I remember. It was a pre–Mother's Day activity at school when we were about six. We'd carefully cut out circles of floral fabric using pinking shears, which left lovely zigzag edges. Jess stuck out her tongue as she always used to, and sometimes still does, when she's concentrating hard. We filled the fabric circles with dried lavender flowers, and the teacher put an elastic band on to secure them before we struggled to tie matching silk ribbons around the top. Both of our mums' bags had exploded in their drawers, scattering bits of dried lavender everywhere. Mum had produced a faded sprig of the purple flower from her bra at the breakfast table one morning, much to Dad's surprise. I smile at the memory and hug Jess tightly, glad to be back with people who know my story without me sharing it. People who understand what Dr. Feld would call "my narrative" without me saying a single word. Back to as normal a life as I can have without Mum. An image of Mum pops into my head, as clear as day, saying one of her catchphrases, "Normal is overrated, Kitty darling."

CHAPTER TWENTY-SEVEN

SHARING IS CARING

Imogen has a sleepover with three of her friends for her fourteenth birthday party, and it's after eleven in the morning when the self-named Glossy Posse finally leaves. Imogen opened her presents while her friends were here, but she didn't touch the cream letter, which has been sitting on the counter all morning. It radiates magnetic waves, and I find myself moving out of my usual chair and sitting in Dad's, which is closer to the letter. I can't wait to read it.

The kitchen table is still overflowing with wrapping paper and ribbons. I'm relieved the envelope isn't at risk of being picked up and thrown into the recycling bin. I wish Imogen would hurry up and open the letter, but she's currently studying her new makeup palette as if it might reveal the secrets of the universe. She finally picks up the envelope and skips off toward the door, ponytail swinging jauntily. Imogen got highlights done for her birthday present from Dad, even though Gran disapproved of her coloring her hair. They catch the light in the sunshine like strands of gold spun for Rumpelstiltskin. I think for the hundredth time how unfair it is that her shiny ponytail looks like a Palomino stallion's and mine looks like Sir Lancelot's stubby tail.

"Imo, wait! Where are you taking the letter?"

"To my room. Ciao."

"Can I read it after you?" I say.

"Nope. Bye."

"But I let you read mine! It's not fair."

Imogen stops and turns around.

"I never asked to read your letter, Kitty. You just passed it around on your birthday and said we could all read it as long as we washed our hands first."

"But still, I let you."

"And I'm not letting you. End of discussion." She looks at Dad with a defiant expression on her face in case he's contemplating intervening. He shrugs.

"It's her letter, Kitty. It's up to her."

As Imogen sets off up the stairs, I yell after her, "Your hair looks yellow, by the way, and you're going to have dark roots when it grows out. You deserve them."

"It's so unfair," I complain to Kate when she takes me to lunch to try to cheer me up the following weekend. "Dad should have made Imogen let me read her letter."

"Your dad's right, Kitty. It is your sister's letter, and you have to respect her choice to keep it private."

"But I let her read my letter. Now it's like she got to hear from Mum twice since she died and I only get to hear from her once. There's no way I'm letting Imogen read my next letter. No way."

Kate studies my face, which is probably scarlet, I'm so angry. The only colors I don't like are the ones that betray my feelings. Dad always says I'd be a terrible poker player. My face turns red when I'm furious, white when I'm shocked, gray when I'm sad, greenish when I'm ill, pink when I'm pleased, and fuchsia when I'm embarrassed.

"Okay, time to go," Kate says, waving to the waiter and miming for him to bring the bill. "Let's head back to my place. It's going to be such fun!"

"What's going to be such fun?" I ask as she bustles me out of the restaurant, waving jauntily to a few of her clients as we leave. Wherever she goes, Kate knows people.

"It's a surprise. Come on. Matt's out at the Arsenal game, so we'll have the apartment to ourselves."

When we get back to Kate's, she heads straight for her desk and produces a compact disc.

"I bet you don't even know what this is," she says. "They were all the rage in my day."

"Of course I do. It's a CD. Mum and Dad have loads. Well, Dad has loads. Which album is it?"

"It's not an album," Kate says, hopping around and looking as if she's about to burst with excitement. "It's a video I found of your mum and me on holiday in America! I was looking for the photos I told you about ages ago, but I'd completely forgotten that there was some video as well."

I gasp. I thought I'd seen every photo and video of Mum. Discovering that there is some new footage is like a lifetime of Christmases and birthdays rolled into one.

We spend the next hour watching and rewatching nineteen-year-old Mum and Kate's adventures in America. In the first clip, Gran is dropping them off at Heathrow airport. Mum and Kate are both wearing enormous backpacks and huge smiles. They are stunningly fresh-faced and absurdly healthy-looking.

Gran is issuing instructions urgently.

"Call twice a week, only use the emergency Visa card in an actual emergency, stay together at all times, no drinking, no smoking, no drugs of any type, don't get into a car with any strange men, actually don't get into a car with any men full stop."

"It's okay, Mum. We'll be sensible. Bye, Dad. Love you."

The camera moves down while Mum hugs the person taking the video.

"Grandpa!" I gasp.

"I know. It's such a shame we don't get to see him in the video. Your grandpa was the best."

Grandpa had died when I was a baby. It suddenly strikes me how terribly sad it is that only two of the four people in this film are still with me. Kate pats my knee.

"Cheer up, Kitty. Next stop, New York City. Oooooh, that rhymes!"

Kate makes me laugh until my sides hurt and tears roll down my cheeks as she tells me stories of their trip and how they'd used the emergency Visa card to buy numerous nonessential items, including denim jackets in NYC, Converse basketball shoes in Chicago, and vintage roller skates in Malibu that wouldn't fit in their backpacks, so they tried to wear them on the plane. Eventually, one of the flight attendants took pity on them and let them go on barefoot, carrying their skates.

"We thought we were so cool. We got into so much trouble with your gran when she got the Visa bill. It took us ages to pay her back!"

"Kate, can you make copies of CDs?"

"I already did—this one's for you. I printed you a copy of the photos of the trip too. Look, this is my favorite."

Kate holds out a picture of Mum standing on a boat, the Statue of Liberty glistening in the background. Mum's pushing her golden hair out of her eyes and grinning from ear to ear. She looks impossibly young and so full of life I can feel the breeze blowing off the water on my cheeks.

"I went on that boat on my first day in New York!" I say.

"I know, your dad told me. He says he has lots of photos of you and your sister on the boat. It would be fun to look at them next to this one. You're starting to look more and more like Laura each day."

"Thanks for today, Kate. You're the best." I hug her. "I can't wait to show the video to Imogen when we get home. Can you stay and watch it with us so you can tell her all the stories you told me?"

"Of course I will." Kate smiles at me fondly. "I knew you'd want to share it with Imogen, even though she didn't let you read her letter. You're such a sweetie."

How could I not share this treasure with my sister? Mum always used to say that sharing is caring. Too bad Imogen has forgotten.

CHAPTER TWENTY-EIGHT

BE MY VALENTINE

I haven't had a Valentine's card since I was seven years old when Toby Kettering, who lived across the street, hand-delivered one to me. He told me proudly that it was the first time his mum had let him cross the road on his own, but she stood outside their house watching the whole time. With his mop of sandy hair, freckles, and winning smile minus his two front teeth, Toby was a real charmer. For weeks afterward, I practiced my signature, writing Kitty Kettering in pink ink and playing weddings with Jess, me as the blushing bride and her the grumpy groom. When Toby and his family moved to Oxford a few months later, Jess consoled me by saying Kitty Kettering sounded like a tongue-twister, but I thought it had a certain ring to it.

Maybe this will be the year I get a real Valentine's

card, preferably from someone with all his front teeth and eyes the color of a green-bean casserole. When Valentine's Day arrives, there's nothing in the mail for me. Imogen gets a card from Josh, which she rips into pieces, takes a picture of, and posts on Instagram. She gets 229 likes. Two days later, though, a white envelope addressed to me appears on the doormat, with an American stamp on it. I tear open the envelope, and a postcard falls out. On one side is a drawing of a smiling rainbow-colored girl with golden-brown eyes standing next to a blue-haired boy with green eyes. I flip the card over, my heart skipping in my chest. On the back of the card is a question mark. It's perfect. Perfectly perfect. I take a picture of the front and back and text it to Jess with lots of smiley faces, love hearts, and exclamation marks.

I know I probably shouldn't give her more reasons to tease me about Henry, but I can't resist telling Imogen about my card that evening. She's always the one with cards lined up on her windowsill at this time of year.

"Do you think I should have sent one to him?" I ask her, as she examines the card, a critical look on her face.

"It's homemade," Imogen says. "How . . . sweet."

"I like it," I say defensively. She can keep her red sparkly store-bought cards. "But do you think I should have sent Henry a card?"

"Did you want to send him one?"

"If I'd known he'd send me one, then I would have done."

"So the answer's no."

"Well, do you think I should text him to say thanks? I mean, it's obvious it's from him. What with the drawing and all."

"Yes. Definitely."

That was a surprisingly helpful conversation with my sister.

"Thanks, Imogen."

"You're welcome. Oh, and Kitty, when you text him, make sure you ask him why he couldn't be bothered to buy a card, and why it was two days late!"

I shut Imogen's door firmly, even though I have some follow-up questions about the timing and contents of the text message. Should I text Henry tomorrow morning so he'll be asleep and I won't be sitting here waiting for a reply, or do I send it now when he's likely to see the message straightaway? I sit down on my bed, consult the clock, and decide to send it now. It's eight o'clock here, so he'll be just getting out of school. Before I start texting, I need to figure out precisely what I'm going to say, and how to reply to a range of potential responses. Otherwise, there'll be awkward pauses where I'm obviously trying to think of what to say. Or worse, the stopping and starting of typing that the recipient can cruelly see on their end—the text equivalent of stuttering. When I've written out the various scenarios and decided on my all-important first text, I begin to type,

"Hi. Kitty here." Best to clarify who I am, just in case he doesn't have my number in his phone anymore. "Just wanted to say thanks for the Valentine's Day card. It's great."

I wait for the response. Half an hour later, still nothing. God, maybe the card was from someone else, but Henry drew it for them. But who else would have sent me a card? After another excruciating hour, my phone chirps.

"👍"

That's it. What am I supposed to say now? While I'm deciding what to write, my phone pings again.

"Good to be back in London?"

That's an easy one.

"Yes."

"Nothing you miss about NYC?" he types.

Ugh, what should I write back?

Thankfully my phone pings again.

"Just finished with my therapist."

"How was that? I am NOT missing Dr. F."

"More Yodaisms! Too bad you're not here. I could tell you all about it."

"What did he say?"

"You will find only what you bring in."

"That's it?"

"That's it."

I consider this piece of wisdom. I actually think I know what the doctor means. Maybe I'm getting good at therapy. Perhaps I've inherited Mum's talents.

"I think I know what that means!" I type.

"Me too. We're becoming experts."

"😊😊😊"

"Well, gotta go. My dad's here causing drama on Broadway."

"Bye."

"Bye, Kitty, let's talk soon . . ."

Henry is text stuttering!

". . . 🩶" he types.

!!!!!!!!!!!!!!!!!

"🩶," I reply.

I fall back onto my pillows, grinning. Wow! Just wow. I grab the Farrow & Ball book of colors that Kate gave me for Christmas and flick through the pages to the pinks. Getting a card from Henry makes me feel like Rangwali, color number 296. I read the description out loud. "This color is exotic, happy, and vital. The most adventurous of our pinks."

"Did Kitty tell you about her Valentine's card?" Imogen asks Kate as we sit around the table for lunch that weekend.

"Imogen, shut up!"

"Oh, I'm sorry, Kitty, don't you want anyone to know about your boyfriend, Henry?"

"He's not my boyfriend," I say, scowling at Imogen.

"And, Kitty's boyfriend has a famous dad," says Imogen, ignoring me and pausing for effect. I'm surprised she doesn't do a drum roll with her knife and fork. "James Davenport."

"No!" says Kate. "James Davenport is absolutely gorgeous! Kitty, why didn't you tell me?"

"Henry is not my boyfriend!"

Kate raises an eyebrow at me. I give a minuscule shrug of my shoulders and try and fail to hide a tiny smile. She grins back. I can tell she wants to jump up and down and ask me loads of questions, but she doesn't. Instead, she turns to Imogen.

"So, Imogen, how many cards did you get this year?"

I relax back in my chair listening to my sister drone on about fancy cards, chocolates, and a dozen red roses, while I think about a handmade card, blue hair, and green bean casserole–colored eyes. Henry's definitely not my boyfriend.

I'll probably never see him again, but maybe, if I did, he would not-not be my boyfriend.

CHAPTER TWENTY-NINE

UNHAPPY ANNIVERSARY

The next big day of the year is one that has been loom-ing for months, but nobody has marked it on the family calendar. Nobody needed to. It's stamped onto each of our hearts.

"I know this is going to be a rough day, girls," says Dad, looking at his watch. "In twelve hours, we can all just collapse on the sofa. How about watching a movie this evening after we go to Primrose Hill? You can choose. We can get pizza too."

We nod mutely. He's trying his best, but the fog is back. The house is Plummett gray again, color number 272. It has always been my least favorite of the Farrow & Ball colors. It's named after the lead weights fisher-men use on their lines. I feel like I have a lead weight around my waist.

"Hello," says Gran, taking off her coat and kissing

each of us, even Dad, which she doesn't usually do except on special occasions, which I suppose this is, in the worst kind of way. She looks fragile and tired. "I thought I'd walk to school with the girls."

"Morning all, only me!" Mrs. Allison appears, Sir Lancelot panting at her heels, and she dumps a big cake tin on the kitchen table. Sir Lancelot's wearing yellow-and-black-striped legwarmers that Mrs. Allison must have made for him to go with his jacket. His legs look like chubby bumblebees. He seems so disgusted with his legwarmers that I feel a small smile pulling at the corners of my mouth. Mrs. Allison notices Dad studying Sir Lancelot, a look of surprise on his face.

"Doesn't he look smashing, Rob?" she says.

"Smashing," says Dad. "We needed a bit of light relief, so thank you both for providing it." He bows at Sir Lancelot, hugs Imogen and me, and heads off to the office.

We walk to school in silence, three abreast, each holding Gran's hand and therefore taking up the entire sidewalk. Gran scowls at approaching pedestrians, who step swiftly into the street to avoid her wrath. She can look quite terrifying, especially if you don't know her. "Cold hands, warm heart" was what Mum always said about her. The sun casts a gentle light on the trees, and birds twitter in their branches, a background track to our melancholy progress to school.

"Kitty, the fox family came back!" says Jessica when I walk into the classroom. Her cheeks are rosy, and she is giddy with excitement. "The babies are teenagers now in fox years. They're not as cute as they were last year, but I'm so happy to see them." She takes a breath and looks at me. "What's up?"

"You don't remember what today is, do you?" I say.

It's not like I expected a card or special treatment, but you'd think my best friend would remember. Jessica puts her head to one side, looking puzzled.

"It's one year today since my mum died," I say, shoving past her and sliding into my seat.

"I'm so sorry, Kitty, I had no idea," she says, and she looks sorry too. "Do you want to come and see the foxes after school?"

"No! I don't want to see your stupid foxes."

Jessica looks as if I'd slapped her, and I feel even more awful. It's not her fault. None of this is her fault.

"Maybe tomorrow?" I say. She nods and rests her hand on my arm.

Primrose Hill is surprisingly busy that evening as we trudge to the top in silence. Dog walkers and runners are taking advantage of the unusually mild weather, and the bench we always sit on is occupied. Imogen and Gran glare at the unsuspecting family as we walk past our spot and sit on the grass, looking down at the city. The sky is an inky blue dotted with pinpricks of stars. The four of us sit quietly, shoulder to shoulder, wrapped up in a cloak of our individual memories. Sentences from Mum's letter, which I know by heart, pop into my mind. "I think of sitting on a star, dangling my bare feet, and I'm so full of love that I swear you will be able to feel it shining down on you . . . I have trillions of light-years of love for you that can never stop shining . . . I love you to the moon and stars and back again."

I'm not sure what I believe happens when you die. Sometimes I can feel Mum so strongly that it takes my breath away. It often happens at random moments, like when I'm buttering toast, or playing with Cleo, or waiting in line for lunch at school. But today, today of all days I can't feel her with me. I stare at the faint stars until my eyes hurt, but there's nothing. She's not here. We stand to leave and brush the grass off our clothes. Without us noticing, the family has left, and our bench is now empty. Who knows how long we sat there, an empty seat behind us?

Imogen and I walk down the hill together, not hand in

hand, but very close. I turn to my sister and see plump tears rolling slowly down her face.

"Imo," I say, and we put our arms around each other. For the first time that day, I cry, heaving great sobs into my sister's shoulder. I cry as if I might never stop.

"I know, I know," she says.

And she does. When Mum was dying, everyone was having their own private experience of losing a daughter or wife or friend, but Imogen and I were going through exactly the same thing at exactly the same time. My big sister was like a mirror for my sadness. She shared my pain and doubled my strength to get through each day. Dad and Gran stand on either side of us, waiting, not wanting to reach into the bubble of grief but wanting to be right there when it bursts. When we pull apart, I look at Dad, and he's half smiling, half crying.

"Mum would be so proud of you both. Seeing the two of you together was always her greatest joy." His voice cracks. "She used to say, 'They'll always have each other, Rob. Long after you and I are gone, the girls will always have each other.'"

My little broken family walks home together. I still can't feel my mum, but I can feel them. That will have to be enough.

* * *

Nobody's in the mood to watch a film when we get home, and nobody has any interest in pizza. Gran makes us each a bowl of soup, which we sit around the table stirring with our spoons until it's an acceptable time to go to bed, and we say good night with relief.

Lying in my room, the Herculean task of making it through the day complete, I think about my smaller memories of Mum. The smaller they are, the more precious they seem, so I always write them down when I remember something new. I worry I'll forget a detail and I might be the only person who knows it. Then it will be gone forever. Who else knows about the time that little sparrow flew into the kitchen window and bounced back onto the terrace, stunned? He lay there, his eyes wide open, shivering. Mum ran inside and grabbed a shoebox, which she lined with an old cardigan, and placed him gently inside. We named him Clunk. When we checked on Clunk for the third time, he'd gone. Mum told me she saw him the next day, reunited with his family and singing cheerily. Thinking about Clunk recovering in his shoebox makes me smile for the first time that day.

I look for more piles of grief glitter that hide smiles—the way Mum used to rub her feet together when she was lying next to me. Or the way she would do funny accents when she read me a story and make me cry with laughter. Or how she used to lie next to me in bed when I was ill, not caring if I coughed and sneezed all over her. She'd hold me close and stroke my hair until I fell asleep.

I sleep.

CHAPTER THIRTY

ACCIDENT AND EMERGENCY

"I just don't get why they're coming to London," I complain for the fifteenth time.

"Probably because it is one of the greatest cities in the world," Dad says.

Jen and Dash are visiting London on a mini tour of Europe. So far they've been to Paris and Rome. We're meeting them for lunch on their third day here. Dad says since Jen did such a lot to make us feel welcome in New York, we have to return the favor.

They're staying in a posh hotel in Knightsbridge, and we arrange to meet them at a restaurant near Kensington Gardens for lunch. When they walk in, I'm transported back to our brunch in New York City all those months ago. This time we're the ones sitting down waiting while Jen and Dash weave their way through the tables to reach us. Well, Jen weaves, and Dash bumps his way.

"Hi, guys!" says Jen. "It's so great to see you, isn't it, Dash?" Her American accent sounds jarring. Jen is looking her usual polished self. Dash is wearing a T-shirt with a Union Jack and the words "Cool Britannia" on it.

"So, so, so great," Dash lisps, taking hold of my hand. He's like a cat who can tell who has allergies and gets right onto their lap.

Dash proceeds to describe his adventures in Europe. He went up the Eiffel Tower, saw a frowning-lady picture (I presume he means the Mona Lisa), and his mum ate a slug—Jen clarifies it was a snail.

"What are you looking forward to seeing in London?" asks Dad. "Buckingham Palace? Big Ben? The Tower of London?"

"We went to the palace yesterday, and my mom said the queen was at home because the flag was flying. Like this one." He points to his T-shirt. "I waved for ages, but I couldn't see her." His face falls. "Do you know the queen, Kitty?" Dash asks, brightening up at the prospect. The kid would actually believe me if I said I do.

"Sorry, Dash, I don't know the queen."

"I saw your boyfriend at school before vacation, Kitty.

He looked sad," Dash says, and I feel my heart give a little flutter.

"I don't have a boyfriend, remember?"

"Yes, you do. Your friend with green hair from the duck game. I like him," Dash says. "His hair is pink now. Why does it keep changing all the time?"

"He means Henry," says Imogen unhelpfully. "So Dash, did Henry look very sad? Missing Kitty?"

"I told him I miss Kitty too," says Dash.

Oh my God! No doubt Dash yelled it across the playground. I can feel the tips of my ears turning pink at the thought of it.

"Henry sent Kitty a Valentine's card," Imogen tells Jen and Dash.

"I got twenty-two Valentine's cards," pipes up Dash. "One from every kid in my grade apart from Sienna. She's not allowed to bring in Valentine's cards because her mom says it's a stupid holiday made up by people who want to sell flowers and chocolates. Zac was supposed to give us each a piece of chocolate, but he ate all of them in the bathroom before class and got sick. His mom had to come and get him from the nurse's office."

"Gosh, what an eventful day for the junior kindergarten class," says Dad and happily changes the subject.

Dash eats his kids' size shepherd's pie, colors in the

picture that the waitress gives him, and plays rock, paper, scissors with Dad before announcing he's bored. Jen should just let him play on her phone like every other parent in the restaurant is doing. Imogen is chatting with Jen about the clothes shops in London compared to New York, and I'm tired of listening to them, so I offer to take Dash to the nearby playground.

"Are you sure you don't mind, Kitty?" says Jen. "That would be awesome."

"Yay!" says Dash, pulling at my hand.

"Make sure you listen to Kitty. She's in charge."

Dash spends a happy ten minutes with me pushing him on the swings and him shouting at me to make him go higher. It's starting to make me feel a bit nervous, so I suggest we go and look at some of the other things to do. There's a climbing wall, and he makes a beeline for it.

"Can I go up it, Kitty?" he asks.

I look at the other kids climbing. Some of them look about Dash's age, so I suppose it's okay.

"Sure," I say, heading to a nearby bench. "I'll watch you from here. Be careful."

Dash skips off and starts climbing up the structure like a mini Spider-Man.

"Not so high, Dash," I say, suddenly feeling nervous as I notice he's managed to get about three feet off the ground in a matter of seconds.

"Kitty!" He lets go of the wall with one hand and waves wildly. "Look at me."

Everything goes into slow motion, and I watch in horror as Dash falls from the wall and hits the ground below with a dull thud. There is a collective intake of breath from the parents and nannies in the playground, and I jump to my feet and run toward him. By the time I reach him, a lady's bending down next to him asking him where it hurts and telling him not to move. Dash's usually flushed cheeks are ashen and one of his legs is unnaturally twisted beneath the other. I reach out to move him into a more comfortable position, but the lady grabs my arm.

"I'm a doctor. We shouldn't move him. John"—she turns to a man standing next to her—"call an ambulance." She swivels back to face me. "Is this your brother? Where are your parents?"

"Kitty, you're here," Dash says, giving me a small smile before closing his eyes.

"He's not my brother." I feel my bottom lip trembling. "I was supposed to be looking after him. His mum's in that café." I point to the nearby restaurant, and stare in silence at Dash. I feel nauseous. After a few minutes, his eyelashes flicker, and he opens his big brown eyes again.

"Where's Mommy?"

Despite what the doctor said about not touching him, I lay my hand very softly on Dash's dark curls, and he closes his eyes again.

"Can I go and get his mum?" I ask the woman.

"Yes, run and get her."

I hear the woman telling Dash that his mummy is on her way and I race across the playground. I fly into the restaurant, heads turning as I clatter into a chair.

"Jen, Dad! Dash fell off the climbing wall. Come quickly!"

Jen leaps to her feet and starts firing questions at me—"What happened, is he okay, who's looking after him?"

When we reach the playground, the ambulance has already arrived. Jen rushes to Dash's side and drops heavily to her knees. It crosses my mind that she will have bruises on her legs later.

"Oh, my baby," she says to Dash, who is now wearing a neck brace. "Is he going to be okay? What happened?" Jen is looking at the medics, but it's Dash who replies.

"Hi, Mommy. I was climbing that wall, and I fell. My leg hurts a lot. This lady's a doctor."

Jen looks at the woman, gratefully.

"We're going to take him to get checked out," one of the paramedics says to Jen. "Looks like a broken leg. He seems fine apart from that, but let's get him to the hospital so they can do some X-rays. You can ride in the ambulance with us, love."

Dash looks so small on the adult-sized stretcher as he's loaded into the back of the ambulance, and I feel the tears welling up in my eyes again.

"Which hospital?" Dad asks the paramedic.

"Chelsea and Westminster."

"We'll be right behind you in a taxi," Dad calls to Jen.

The second the ambulance pulls away, I burst into tears. Imogen appears looking flustered.

"Dad, you left without paying!" she says.

Dad passes Imogen a wad of notes and instructs her to pay and then head home while we go to the hospital.

"It's okay, love," says Dad. "Come on, let's get a taxi, and you can tell me what happened on the way to the hospital."

Four hours and a gazillion tests later, Dash is given the all-clear to go home. He has a broken leg, an egg-sized bump on his head, and is very pleased with his neon-green cast. He got to choose the color himself.

Despite both Dad and Jen assuring me that it wasn't my fault, that accidents happen, and that Dash is absolutely fine and will have an exciting London story to tell when he gets back to school, I feel awful. Jen is being kind, but I'm sure she must hate me. I would.

We take Jen and Dash back to their hotel and get them settled. Jen orders room service for the two of them and sets Dash up on the big bed with his iPad and says that he can watch *Dora* until their food arrives.

"Anything we can do?" Dad asks.

"No, I don't think so, Rob."

"Well, call me if you need anything. Maybe you should come and hang out at our place tomorrow. Better than staying at the hotel all day, and Dash could probably do with a day off sightseeing."

I'm pretty sure the last place Jen will want to be is at our house, but she smiles and says that would be great.

"I'll just say goodbye to Dash," I say and walk over to the bed. The iPad has fallen onto his chest, and his eyes are closed. I bend and give him a gentle kiss on the cheek.

"I'm so sorry, Dash," I whisper. He really is quite sweet when he's asleep.

He opens his eyes and smiles at me.

"Don't be sad, Kitty," he says before closing them again.

The next morning at breakfast, I'm moping around the kitchen. Imogen says my self-flagellation—a word I need to go and look up—is getting really tedious, and given Jen doesn't blame me, why am I still talking about it? Soon after Jen and Dash arrive at our house, Mrs. Allison appears with Sir Lancelot and a batch of her fantastic blueberry and lemon muffins. Dash immediately lies down on the floor next to Sir Lancelot and presses his button nose into Sir Lancelot's fur.

"I love you," I hear him whispering.

"Oh, and he loves you too, poppet," says Mrs. Allison. "Now, are you feeling well enough to do some baking with me later?"

"Yes!" says Dash. "What are we going to make?"

"Dog treats for Sir Lancelot," Mrs. Allison says, grinning broadly. "We'll shape them like little bones."

"What do they taste like?"

"You know, I've never tried one. Sir Lancelot loves them. I have to remember not to bake them for too long, as he's not very good at crunching things anymore. He likes them on the softer side."

"How do we make them?"

"Peanut butter, eggs, pumpkin puree, and whole-wheat flour."

"Yummy! Can I try one?" Dash asks.

"I don't see why not," says Mrs. Allison. "If it's okay with your mummy."

"Why not?" says Jen weakly.

I'm sure she didn't imagine her son having a broken leg or eating dog treats on his trip to Europe.

"How about we go out for lunch?" asks Dad.

"I don't want to," Dash says. "I want to watch TV. *Peppa Pig*'s my new favorite show. Her voice sounds like yours, Kitty."

Imogen snorts with laughter.

"You sound like Daddy Pig, Imogen," Dash says delightedly. It's my turn to snort.

"Dash can stay here with me if you and Jen want to go out," says Imogen. "I've got homework to do, and I'll make sure Kitty doesn't break his other leg."

"Very funny, Imogen," Dad says. "Well, what do you think, Jen? There's a lovely Greek restaurant just around the corner, so we wouldn't be far." Jen looks doubtful. I knew she hadn't forgiven me!

"I'm happy to stay with him as well," says Mrs. Allison. "Sir Lancelot and I are free this afternoon."

"Yay!" says Dash. "Sir Lancelot can watch *Peppa Pig* with me."

"Well, that would be lovely, if you're sure you don't mind," Jen says to Imogen and Mrs. Allison. Clearly, my services as a babysitter are no longer required. I scowl. I'm still upset about what happened with Dash yesterday, and now Dad and Jen are going out for lunch alone.

Dash settles down happily in front of *Peppa Pig* with a blueberry muffin, a cup of milk, and Sir Lancelot, who Mrs. Allison heaved onto the sofa—"just this once, mind," she said. "A special treat because of your leg."

"Imogen," I hiss. "Why on earth did you suggest Dad and Jen go out for lunch?"

"Why not? It's Jen's last day in London. No point in us all sitting around here, is there?"

"It just seems weird, the two of them going out on their own like that."

"Oh my God, Kitty. You don't still think they're going to start dating, do you? They live on opposite sides of the Atlantic."

"Hmmm," I say, still suspicious. "Well, I don't like it, plus if any of the neighbors see Dad with a strange woman, they'll think he's got a girlfriend."

"You need to stop worrying about what a bunch of random, nosy neighbors might think. Now be quiet and fetch me a muffin. I want to watch *Peppa Pig*."

"Get your own muffin."

Gran arrives just as the third episode of *Peppa* is ending.

"Was that your father and Jennifer I just saw in the Greek restaurant?" she asks.

I've noticed before that Gran calls Dad "your father" when she's annoyed with him.

"Yup," Imogen says. "Dad's taken her out for lunch as it's her last day."

"Hmmm," says Gran. "Seems strange."

"Exactly what I said," I say.

Gran and I exchange loaded glances. It's a good thing Jen and Dash are flying back to New York tomorrow. I feel guilty every time I look at Dash's neon cast, and I really don't want my dad and Jen going out for any more lunches. Luckily there's an ocean between them, and nothing can remove the Atlantic. You know what they say, out of sight, out of mind.

CHAPTER THIRTY-ONE

HOME IS WHERE THE HEART IS

"Girls, there's something I want to discuss with you," Dad says a month later. He sounds excited.

Oh great, here we go. What now? It is almost certainly going to be something that I'm not going to like one bit. He looks at us to make sure that we're both paying attention. We are.

"How do you feel about moving back to New York—for a couple of years this time? My boss is keen that I go back to oversee the project I started there. It's fully funded now, so it would be great, sort of like running my own small business."

"Fine by me," says Imogen, sounding as relaxed as if Dad had just suggested going to the movies that evening. "I'm so over London. At least in New York, I won't have to see Josh and Scarlett slobbering all over each other outside Starbucks. It's gross. Plus, I can't stand having to wear a school uniform. Can Lily come and stay?"

I look at Dad to see if he thinks that avoiding seeing your ex-boyfriend kissing Scarlett Wilson is a good reason to move to the other side of the world, but he's just smiling at Imogen—a bemused look on his face. Imogen continues to blather on about how Josh sucks, and how Lily heard from another girl that Scarlett is going to dump Josh soon anyway and that he'd better not expect Imogen to offer him a shoulder to cry on. I gaze out of the window at the familiar garden, the feel of the worn wooden kitchen table warm under my hands. I know every groove of its surface. There isn't a single thing that I know every groove of in New York. There I was like a fish out of water. Home is where the heart is, and my heart's in London with Gran, Kate, Jess, Mrs. Allison, and Cleo. There was something about being in New York, though, something that I didn't even know I needed—I could walk down any street and into any room without seeing a Mum-shaped gap.

"Kitty?" Dad says, interrupting my reverie. He's looking at me and crinkling up his forehead in a worried way. "What do you think?"

"I don't know. We've only been home for six months. We can't keep ping-ponging across the Atlantic." The idea of it is making me feel tired.

"We're not going to ping-pong, Kitty. Last time we

were in New York was more like an extended holiday. This time we'd really get the opportunity to experience living there. Don't you think that would be fun?"

Dad looks excited, but I just shrug.

"Well, we don't need to decide right away. Let's take some time to think about it. On the positive, it would be brilliant for my career, a big step up. Do you have any questions about the move?"

I shake my head. The question I don't want the answer to is whether this has anything to do with Jen.

I decide not to tell Jess about New York. I don't want to upset her, and somehow if I don't talk about it, we're less likely to have to move.

"Guess what," Jess says as we walk through the school gates the next morning.

"What?"

"We're moving."

I stop and turn to face her. "You're what? Why? Where? When?"

"My parents are sick of not having enough space in our house, so we're moving to Hampshire this summer."

"But you won't be able to come to Haverstock Girls' School from Hampshire, will you?" I'm not sure exactly how far away Hampshire is, but it's definitely not close enough for her to come here every day.

"No, silly. I'll be starting a new school—one with actual boys. Finally, I'll have a chance of getting a boyfriend before I'm twenty."

"You're happy about moving?" I ask, feeling strangely betrayed.

"Mostly. I mean, I'll miss you, obviously, but it's only an hour and a half on the train, and Mum says you can come and stay for the weekend whenever you like."

"That's not the same, though."

"No," Jess agrees, "but guess what else."

"What?"

"I'm getting a horse!" Jess's face is glowing with excitement, and her eyes are shining. For as long as I've known her, she's been horse mad. When we were little, we used to canter around the playground, with her holding a rope around my waist and shouting giddy-up. She spends every weekend taking riding lessons and hanging out at the stables. She even shovels horse poo voluntarily. It's the one thing we don't share. Horses scare me, and who in their right mind wants to pick up poo?

"Jess, that's amazing," I say, and I hug her. I mean it—I'm happy for her, and we hold on to each other and jump up and down, just the way we used to when we were younger and our mums agreed we could have a sleepover.

"I know, I can't believe it! Can you believe it, Kitty?"

As Jess chatters on excitedly about her new horse that she's going to name Cinnamon, I look around the playground and think about school without Jess. I can't believe it, and I can't imagine being here without her. I wonder if Dad would consider moving to Hampshire instead of New York.

"Jess is moving to Hampshire," I announce to Gran when I get home from school, dumping my bag on the floor. I still can't get my head around it.

"Is she now?" Gran says. "And how does Jess feel about that?"

"She's mostly happy. She's getting a horse, she'll be going to a school with boys, and she'll have a huge bedroom for when I come to visit." Jess and I always joke that her current room is the size of Harry Potter's cupboard under the stairs.

"You'll miss her," says Gran, stirring her cup of tea.

"It's not going to be the same without her," I say. "She's always been at school with me. Why do things have to keep changing, Gran?"

"'The only constant in life is change,'" says Gran.

"Was it Heraclitus who said that, Kitty?"

"I think so," I say. I have no idea who Heraclitus is, but Gran is usually right.

"So your dad told me he'd talked to you and your sister about moving back to New York for a few years. What do you think about that?"

"I don't know."

"Shall we make a list of pros and cons?" she asks. Gran is a big list maker.

"Sure."

"Excellent, you speak, and I'll take notes."

Gran pulls an envelope out of the recycling tray in front of her and looks at me expectantly.

"I always like to start with the cons and get them out of the way," she says. "Sort of like with good news, bad news—who would choose good news first?"

"Mum used to," I say.

Gran smiles. "So she did. Well, how about you?"

"Cons—I'd have to leave everyone I love—you, Kate, Jess, Mrs. Allison, and Cleo."

Gran notes it down in her small, neat handwriting and looks up at me.

"Um . . . well, we only just moved back, and I feel like a Ping-Pong ball."

Gran writes down Ping-Pong.

"What else, Kitty?"

"Jen," I say, and Gran raises an eyebrow, pushing her pen firmly into the paper.

"Care to elaborate?"

"Not really."

"All right. What else should be on the list?"

"We'd have to leave our house and go and live in some random apartment again—probably one with all-white walls. I'd have to go back to that school, and that would be weird and embarrassing." I'm working up quite a head of steam now, the words tumbling out and Gran scribbling to catch up with me.

"Excellent. Any other cons?"

"Definitely, but I can't think of them at the moment."

"Okay, we can come back to them. Pros?"

I close my eyes and picture New York City and feel something like excitement fluttering in my chest. Images of steam pouring out from manhole covers in the streets, a sky so bright even on the coldest January days, a line of yellow cabs stretching down Broadway, a glimpse of the silver scales of the Chrysler building, like a giant herring standing on its tail, and a smiling boy with blue hair fizz through my mind. I imagine casually texting Henry to tell him I'll be back in New York in September.

"Well? Are there any?" Gran says.

"It's New York," I say.

"Is that it?"

"Yes, but that's quite a lot."

Gran writes down New York in big letters, sets the pen down, and smiles at me, as if she knows something important that I don't.

Gran joins us for Sunday night's family meeting. There are two agenda items: (1) Why does Imogen generate more laundry than a small village? (2) Should we move back to New York? Item one is quickly dealt with as Imogen reluctantly agrees she has to do her own laundry from now on. We move onto agenda item two.

"So, Kitty, Gran told me all about your list, we had a bit of a chat about it, and Eleanor has an idea to propose."

I look at Gran. I hope she didn't show Dad the comment about Jen. Gran gives a tiny shake of her head. Phew!

"Thank you, Rob," Gran says. "So, girls, what do you think of me coming to New York with you for the first three months?"

I look at Gran in surprise.

"You'd come with us?"

"Yes. I rather like the idea of spending longer in New York. I'd forgotten how much I enjoy being there until I visited you. Plus, I thought it might help you settle in."

"What about Cleo? Who'll look after her if you're coming to New York?"

"That's something else that we discussed," says Dad. "Cleo could come to New York with us. She can get a passport for pets and wouldn't even need to go into quarantine. Kate, Jess, and Mrs. Allison can all come and visit."

"Oh," I say, watching my objections to New York float off into the air like little puffs of smoke—Jess is leaving London, Gran, and even Cleo would come with us to New York. Kate and Mrs. Allison could visit us. New York is like a cool new kid at school named Delilah or Dylan—intimidating and quite likely to get you into trouble, but hard to ignore. London is like a sensible older cousin, a Victoria or perhaps a Charlotte, very dependable, very comforting, very safe, but a tiny bit dull in the nicest possible way because you've known her forever. I look around the table at Dad, Imogen, and Gran. Cleo pops her sooty little face up from her place on Gran's lap and looks at me expectantly.

"Well, Kitty?" says Dad.

Well indeed.

CHAPTER THIRTY-TWO

TWELVE TODAY

The birds bickering in the branches outside my window wake me before six. I stretch out on my comfy bed, dislodging Cleo, who has been sleeping in the crook of my knees. She gives me a friendly look, twitches one ear, and closes her eyes again. It seems like much longer than a year since I woke up in the Peony room at Kate's house with Pasha glaring at me on my eleventh birthday. Cleo is much friendlier, unless you're Sir Lancelot—then she definitely has a touch of Pasha.

Cleo follows me downstairs and into the kitchen, which is crowded with packing boxes. She leaps gracefully onto the tallest box, and I weave around it to kiss Dad. Just like last year, he's sitting at the table drinking a cup of tea, this time from the mug I gave him for Father's Day that reads "Dad, you are TEA-rrific!" Annoyingly, Imogen bought him a mug too, even though

I had already told her I was getting him one. Hers reads "From your FAVORITE daughter." Very funny.

"Happy birthday, Kitty!" Dad says, standing up to hug me. "It's a gorgeous day. Shall we have breakfast outside?"

"Sounds great, but first I'm going to read Mum's letter."

I grab the cream envelope from the pile laid out at my usual place at the table and skip outside. The grass is wet with dew and feels deliciously fresh underneath my bare feet. At the end of the lawn is the tree house. *Tree house* may be an overstatement since it's more of a platform with a slanted roof wedged between the garden wall and the elm tree. It used to seem so high when I first climbed into it, but I could probably easily jump down now. On second thought, maybe it's still a little high for that. The tree house was already here when we moved in, and Dad always had big plans to upgrade it, which never happened. I like it as it is. There's a wonky old deck chair up there, which I gingerly sit down in, and I carefully open the envelope. As I unfold the letter, the little tissue paper package spills onto my lap. The wrapping paper this year is the palest green, like the inside of a cucumber. I hold the letter to my lips for a minute, knowing Mum's hands were the last to touch it, take a deep breath, and begin to read.

My darling Kitty,

Happy, happy birthday, my beautiful, brilliant girl! I love you more than words can say. Twelve already! That was a big year for me. I got the lead part in the school play and threw up just before I went on stage because I was so nervous on the first night. I fell off a horse named Russell and broke my arm. Russell was such a pathetic horse name, I called him Thunder when I told people the story. I failed my flute exam. I had a crush on John Taylor from Duran Duran—google him—you'll laugh so much when you see his hair. Best of all, it was the year I met my beautiful, beloved Kate. She was the best friend I didn't even realize I was missing until I found her. Give her a massive kiss from me and tell her how much I love her. I'm so glad she's your fairy godmother.

For your twelfth birthday, I chose a hummingbird charm for you to add to your bracelet. Do you remember when we saw the hummingbirds on holiday in Costa Rica a few years ago? You and I watched them for hours while Dad and Imo went zip-lining. They were iridescent blues and greens, and you said that nobody could ever make paint to match that color so we should do our best to remember it always.

Here are some things I learned about
hummingbirds when I was choosing your charm.

1. They can visit 1,000 flowers a day,
   and they always remember which ones
   they've been to and how long each flower
   takes to refill with nectar.
2. They flap their wings seventy times a
   second.
3. They can fly in six directions: up, down,
   left, right, forward, and backward.
4. They are the tiniest birds in the world
   and weigh less than a penny.
5. Their favorite color is red.

Hummingbirds are symbols of living life in
the moment and of being adaptable. Memories can
be beautiful things, Kitty, but I want you to live
for today. Always remember how much I love you,
but never let your memories hold you back. What I
hope for the people I love is that they live and love to
the fullest. That means you will need to try new
things, visit new places, and meet new people. You
might fall, you might fail, and you might feel so
nervous that you want to run away or throw up, or

both, but don't be afraid to try. Never be afraid to try.

There'll be times when you wish everything could stay the same, and other times when you pray for everything to be different. The only sure thing in life is change, so you should try to embrace it. Turning your back won't stop it from happening. I know you can look it right in the eye. You, Imogen, and Dad will all have changed by now, and you'll keep growing and evolving as the weeks, months, and years pass. That will be wonderful but also hard sometimes. Be each other's biggest fans. Embrace life, love, and especially each other.

I'm almost at the end of my allotted pages, and Dad is sitting here keeping a close eye on me, so I'll say goodbye for now. Keep looking for happiness like the hummingbirds look for nectar and don't be afraid to change direction as needed.

Adventure awaits, my darling Kitty.

Love forever,

Mum xxx

I lie back in the deck chair, feeling the growing warmth of the July sun stroke my face, and fasten the little silver hummingbird to my bracelet. Stretching my arms up to the sky, I watch the hummingbird hover between the heart and the star. The ruby sparkles in the morning sun, and I smile because Mum just said that red was the hummingbird's favorite color, and I can still learn new things from her, even now. The world hasn't stopped after I read the letter like it did last year. I can still hear the bees busily buzzing around the lavender pots below the tree house, the birds singing in the branches above me, and Sir Lancelot barking in the garden next door. My insides feel soft, warm, and golden, and I realize that the feeling I have inside me is peace. I close my eyes and think about what Mum had written. She always told me it was okay to be nervous as long as I didn't let that stop me from doing new things. She'd be happy we've decided we are going to live in New York, happy that we're having adventures, happy that we haven't tried to freeze time. I lie there for another ten minutes, until Dad calls me in for breakfast. I daringly hop down from the tree house without using the ladder and skip inside to show Imogen and Dad my hummingbird. Adventure awaits!

CHAPTER THIRTY-THREE

WAITING AT THE SAME WINDOW

The street is bright and busy on this August morning, and the birds are cheerfully welcoming the start of a new day. I peek at them among the glossy leaves of the tree outside my window. It needs pruning; the branches are almost touching the glass. I check the Farrow & Ball color chart before I take it off my wall, my eyes searching for the perfect match until they land on number 287, Yeabridge Green. The sunlight pouring through the window catches the wings of the hummingbird charm on my bracelet. Its tiny silver wings have intricate lines etched on them, making the creature look as if it has feathers and might take flight if you don't watch it carefully.

"Kitty, the van will be here in a minute. Are you ready?" yells Dad up the stairs.

"Almost," I call, glancing around my bedroom. The

bed has been stripped, the sheets, duvet, and pillows packed away, ready to go into storage along with the furniture and the books, games, and pictures I'm leaving behind. The walls will be painted tomorrow. The real estate agent says that while the kaleidoscope of colors I have on my walls is unique, rental properties should be neutral. The real estate agent picked the paint. The color he chose is unimaginatively named "off-white" and does what it says on the can. Imogen is excited to get more Imogen's Ice Cream to put on the walls in her room in New York. I'll have to go back to see Mike to get some more paint made.

It is a year and a half since I stood at this window waiting for the black car to arrive to take us to the church. Twinkle and my favorite photograph are the only things left to put into my backpack. I study the framed picture of Mum with the Statue of Liberty, tracing my finger gently over the joyful face of the nineteen-year-old girl smiling fearlessly back at the whole world from the photograph, and I grin. She would smile just like that if I could tell her we are going to New York.

I've found little piles of grief glitter all over this room, this house, and this city, but I've realized it will go everywhere with me, and that's okay. The glitter is the memories. It does get everywhere, but it contains every color—the happy pinks and reds, the flecks of blue and lilac that make your heart overflow with joy, as well as the gold and silver that might bring you to your knees. When the specks are mixed together, glitter makes a unique color that you can't possibly begin to describe. I read somewhere that grief is love with nowhere to go, but my happy and sad thoughts about Mum all sit together now. I don't need to hide from the grief glitter anymore or try to sweep it away.

Through the window, I see the white moving van turn onto the street. It looks as if it might not fit, and I think about how awful it would be if the driver scraped Mrs. Allison's new cherry-red Renault, bought with the proceeds of her best-selling book, *The Cake Lady*. Mrs. Allison dedicated the book to Sir Lancelot, Imogen, and Kitty. I'm sure she only added Imogen's name so that my sister wouldn't feel left out. I'm definitely her favorite Wentworth. All of our furniture is being delivered to a storage unit outside London, so the freshly painted house will be ready for the new tenants to move in next week. They've signed a two-year lease. I put the photo and Twinkle into my bag and head for the door. Glancing over my shoulder to check that Imogen isn't watching me, I say goodbye to the cherry tree and its tuneful feathery residents, goodbye to my room, goodbye to this house. I'm really not sure when we will be back, but I don't need to say goodbye to Mum. I know she's coming with me on my next adventure.

It's time to go.

ACKNOWLEDGMENTS

Saying thank you is always fun, so here goes.

The biggest thank you of all is to the three people with whom I share my every day—Abel, Beatrice, and Gabriel—for your love, support, and complete confidence in me each step of the way. None of this would be possible without the three of you.

Thank you to my mum and dad for filling my world with books from the very start and to Fay for being the best big sister imaginable—how lucky I am to have had you in my life from day one.

Thank you to my brilliant friends on both sides of the Atlantic for reading the earliest versions of Kitty's story and providing love, laughter, encouragement, and a shoulder along the way. I am so grateful to know you'll always be in my corner. Special thanks to my youngest supporter, Arianna, for reading the manuscript over ten

My profound gratitude goes to agent extraordinaire Elizabeth Bewley at Sterling Lord Literistic for rescuing Kitty from a mountain of manuscripts and being such a delightful and incredibly capable guide on this wonderful journey.

Thank you to super editor Tara Weikum for loving Kitty's story, conjuring the words into an actual book, and being a joy to work with at each stage of the process. I am so grateful to the talented and dedicated team at HarperCollins, including Sarah Homer, Emma Meyer, Jessie Gang, Nicole Moreno, and Anna Bernard. And many thanks to Oriol Vidal for creating this gorgeous cover, which Kitty would love so much.

And to all of you reading my book—thank you.

Don't miss this sneak peek of

THE
HOUSE
SWAP

the next novel from Yvette Clark!

PART ONE
HOME

CHAPTER ONE

Allie

IS AT CRINGLE COTTAGE, OXFORDSHIRE, ENGLAND

"I knew it! Middle child syndrome is officially a thing. I sent my parents an article about it that I found on the Good Parents Make Great Kids website. They haven't read it." (from my diary)

The fingerprint in the talcum powder I sprinkled on the handle of my desk drawer this morning proves it—someone has been going through my stuff. I read about the talcum powder technique in a book called *Think Like a Spy*. Ms. Leonard said I could keep it for the summer, even though I already had the maximum number of books from the school library.

I take a picture with my phone and zoom in on it, but I can't tell if the fingerprint is a loop or a whorl. *Think Like a Spy* says that there are three main types of fingerprint patterns: the loop, the whorl, and the arch. I have an arch print—it's the rarest kind. Only 5 percent of the population have it, so if you are a criminal, the arch is the worst type of print to have. I don't plan on being a criminal. I want to be a spy when I'm older. I doubt having arch fingerprints is a barrier to becoming a spy. If it is, maybe I could have plastic surgery on my fingertips. I make a mental note to look it up later.

My sister, Willow, has a loop print. I know this because I took her fingerprints last week. I suggested that we make a handprint painting of Chickpea, Nestle, and Nugget to decorate their hen house. I could tell that Mum was surprised that I'd volunteered to do something with my little sister for a change—surprised and pleased because Willow is a lot of work. Willow pressed her palm onto a plate of white paint and pushed it down on the paper to make the chicken's body, then she painted a yellow beak at the side of her thumbprint, a red crest on the top of the thumbprint, and drew tiny black eyes, black legs, and red feet with a marker. She was very proud of it. The picture's not on the wall of The Chick-Inn yet because Willow's taking it around the village to show everyone whether they want to see it or not.

I'm not sure how I'm going to get my brother's prints, but I'll think of something. It will be just my luck if Max has a loop print too. He probably does because it's the most common kind. His prints will be much bigger than

Willow's, though, so it should be easy to tell them apart. I took Mum and Dad's prints, too—they're both whorls. I wonder if you are more likely to marry someone who has the same fingerprint type as you. Maybe I should try to get Toby South's prints when we go back to school. How would I even do that? Imagine if he caught me trying to get his prints from his locker. I'd die.

Even dogs have prints—not on their paws, though, on their noses. Bear didn't seem to mind me taking his nose print at all. I think he liked the taste of the food coloring I used to do it. He kept licking it off, so it took a long time to get a clear print.

I can't decide who the number one suspect for snooping around in my desk drawer is—Max or Willow. They both have reasons to go through my stuff. Max to find something he could use to embarrass or blackmail me, like my diary or a letter from a boyfriend, as if I'd ever risk keeping my diary in our house with a brother like him, and I've never even had a boyfriend. And Willow because she is a thief, which my parents don't seem concerned about for some reason.

"Well, she didn't actually take anything," Dad said after I caught Willow trying to crack the combination lock on my money-box.

"Only because she couldn't get it open! Why aren't you

and Mum worried about this? Did you even read that article I gave you?"

After I found the calligraphy set that I got for my birthday under Willow's pillow a few weeks ago, I printed out an article called "Is My Child a Kleptomaniac?" from the Good Parents Make Great Kids website and presented it to my parents.

"Actually, I did, and it said it's a completely normal phase for a six-year-old," Dad said. "Relax! Also, did you sign me up for newsletters from that website? I keep getting random emails from them."

I don't think it's a completely normal phase, and I hate it when people tell me to relax. Maybe I could relax if my parents paid a bit more attention to what my brother and sister get up to. Maybe then I wouldn't have to sign them up for the Good Parents Make Great Kids newsletter. Mum and Dad believe in free-range parenting, which is good for our chickens but not for my siblings.

In addition to their casual approach to parenting, my parents didn't seem to give much thought to naming their kids. I guess Allegra is slightly better than Willow, but weirdly, the name suits her. I don't know what name would suit me, but it is definitely not Allegra. Fifty babies born in England last year were named Allegra, which is fifty too many if you ask me. Thank

4

goodness everyone calls me Allie. Well, everyone except Max because he knows that I hate being called Allegra. I asked Mum what on earth they were thinking when they gave me that name.

"Allegra is a gorgeous name, Allie," she said, looking offended. "It was always top of our list, wasn't it, Angus?"

I dread to think what else was on the list. Mum takes it very personally that I don't love my name, even though I'm the one that's stuck with it. I pointed out that even she and Dad mostly call me Allie, except when they're annoyed with me and call me by my full name—Allegra Iris Greenwood—like when I won't play with my sister. I wonder if anyone ever got a restraining order against a six-year-old.

"Allegra's the name of an allergy medicine," Max said. "Side effects include being annoying, boring, and stupid."

"Actually, the name means joyful," Mum said.

Max snorted. I think I might be allergic to my brother, and there's no medicine for that.

"Anyway, Allie," Mum said, ignoring Max, "we wanted to give you a beautiful and unusual name. There were so many Emmas at my class that at least five people answered whenever the teacher said Emma. I had to be

5

called Emma V. Only one of us got to be just Emma, but she ended up being called Just Emma, so Emma V. was probably better."

"Allegra is unusual," Dad said.

"Just not beautiful," Max said, smirking. "It really suits you, Allegra."

"Shut up, Maximilian Constantine," I said, which wiped the annoying smirk off his face. He hates being called Maximilian, especially if I add his middle name.

"You shut up."

"You suck."

"You suck more."

I punched his arm. "Idiot."

He kicked my leg. "Loser."

Mum rolled her eyes. She always says that we'll grow out of our bickering eventually and become great friends.

We won't.

CHAPTER TWO

Sage

IS AT CANYON VIEW, CALIFORNIA, USA

"Often called the 'heart stone,' rose quartz is the crystal of unconditional love. Do you need to protect and grow the love around you? If so, this is the crystal for you." (from *Crystals A–Z*)

The guest rooms are just as perfect as they are each morning—the white comforters and pillows like freshly fallen snow. Nobody slept in here last night, that's for sure. I close the door behind me and exhale. Maybe I don't need to worry after all.

"Good morning, sweetie," Mom says, appearing from my parents' bedroom. "What are you doing in there?"

"Um, I heard Pandora meowing," I say, trying to ignore the fact that I can clearly see Pandora delicately washing a white paw at the top of the stairs. "I thought she might have gotten shut in there. Oh, wait, there she is."

I point in Pandora's direction. Mom and the cat study me suspiciously.

I started checking the guest rooms a few months ago after my friend Nora told me that her dad sleeping in the guest room was when she and her brother knew for sure that their parents were getting divorced. I set my alarm clock for six a.m. every morning, so I can check. I have no clue what I'd say if I did find one of them asleep in a guest room. Maybe I should stop checking bedrooms and just ask my parents what's going on. They always say I can talk to them about anything, but the words stick in my throat like a fishbone. Maybe I don't want to know the truth. Maybe I already do. Maybe if I ask what's wrong with them, just by saying the words aloud, by putting it out into the universe, I'll make it happen.

Every day my parents act more and more polite around each other, and the more polite they get, the more worried I am. I miss their silly bickering, which always used to end in apologies, hugs, and often way too much kissing. Now they tiptoe around each other, and our house is as quiet as a library at midnight. I touch the white walls of the hallway, imagining the laughter that has soaked into them over the years. The quieter the house gets, the quieter I become. I wish for the thousandth time that I had a brother or sister to talk to about my parents—our parents. Somebody who would understand that when

Mom and Dad are in the same room, even though they still smile at each other, it feels like someone has turned up the air conditioning.

"You look very serious this morning," Mom says, tucking my hair gently behind my ear. "How about some breakfast?"

"Is Dad up?"

"Not yet. He was working late last night. He'll probably sleep in."

"I can wait."

"Well, I can't—my stomach's growling. Come on, let's go eat," Mom says, steering me toward the stairs.

We always used to eat breakfast as a family on weekends. We'd make waffles, never pancakes, because Dad doesn't like them. We'd stack the waffles so high that they looked like the Leaning Tower of Pisa, top them with juicy blueberries, raspberries, and wafer-thin slices of banana, and then drench them with maple syrup. Dad explained that the Leaning Tower of Pisa doesn't fall over because its center of gravity is within the width of its base. He drew a diagram for me. Dad's an architect and is always teaching me interesting stuff like that. He says he thinks of everything in terms of shapes. When I was little, Dad used to describe our family as a perfect triangle with me standing safely balanced on the pinnacle and him and Mom smiling up at me from the bottom corners. Our triangle family was always an equilateral triangle in his drawings, but lately, we feel like a sad scalene triangle with all different angles.

When we get to the kitchen, Mom starts bustling around, pulling eggs, berries, milk, and juice out of the fridge while I sit watching her, rubbing the rose quartz crystal I keep in my pocket with my thumb. It's a raw crystal, which means it's exactly the way it was when it came out of the ground—the edges haven't been smoothed and polished. The pale pink stone looks like a shard of ice, and you'd think the ridges would feel sharp and cold, but the crystal is smooth and warm. My friend Nora prefers the smooth, shiny tumbled stones, but there's something about the texture of this crystal that's comforting.

"Which one is it today?" Mom asks, smiling.

"Rose quartz," I say, holding up the crystal to show her.

"Pretty."

"It's called the heart stone. It's supposed to help with love and stuff."

Mom looks at me in surprise. "Is there someone you like at school you haven't told me about?"

"No!"

Mom smiles like she doesn't believe me. I don't tell her why I'm really carrying this particular crystal around, why it's the one I always have with me now, and why I've hidden small rose quartz crystals around the house, down the side of the sofa, and in their bedroom.

"Earth to Sage! Can I get some help here?"

"Why does Dad have to work all the time?" I ask, not moving.

"He's really busy with that pitch for the hotel project in New York."

"Well, since I'm sleeping over at the twins' house after their party, maybe Dad could not work tonight, and you two could go out for dinner or to a movie or something."

"Maybe," she says, cracking another egg. She hands me the bowl and a fork. "Here you go. Whisk."

"It's been forever since you guys have been out, just the two of you."

I don't want to whisk. I want to tell Mom that if they went out and talked and laughed like they used to do, maybe our angles would be equal again. We might get back to being sixty degrees each.

"How about pancakes for a change?" Mom asks brightly.

"Dad hates pancakes."

"Dad's asleep."

Suddenly I'm not hungry.